WHEN MISCHIEF CAME TO TOWN

WHEN MISCHIEF CAME TO TOWN

By Katrina Nannestad

Houghton Mifflin Harcourt
Boston New York

www.hmhco.com

The text was set in Adobe Garamond.

Library of Congress Cataloging-in-Publication Data
Nannestad, Katrina.
When mischief came to town / by Katrina Nannestad.
p. cm.
Summary: In 1911, when orphaned ten-year-old Inge comes to live with
her stern grandmother in a remote island village in Bornholm, Denmark,
she ends up changing the climate of the town, bringing joy and laughter
to her grandmother's life and finding a new family for herself to
help assuage her grief over losing her mother.
ISBN 978-0-544-53432-2
[1. Orphans—Fiction. 2. Grandmothers—Fiction. 3. Behavior—Fiction.
4. Grief—Fiction. 5. Bornholm (Denmark)— History—20th century—
Fiction. 6. Denmark—History—20th century—Fiction.] I. Title.
PZ7.1.N36Wh 2015
[Fic]—dc23
2014028513

Manufactured in the United States of America
DOC 10 9 8 7 6 5 4 3 2 1
4500567124

For the Great Dane,
who introduced me to the land of
Hans Christian Andersen fairy tales,
pickled herring, hop dancing, and winter barns
filled with squealing piglets and docile cows

Every man's life is a fairy tale, written by God's fingers.

— HANS CHRISTIAN ANDERSEN

CONTENTS

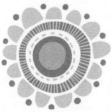

1911
Bornholm
Denmark

Chapter 1

THE GRATEFUL GOAT AND
THE TALKING SPOONS

Here I am, feeling sorry for myself.

I'm sitting on a wooden crate, wedged between a cage full of geese and a goat. If I press too hard against the geese, they honk and peck at me, and even though my coat is too thick for it to hurt, it makes me want to cry. If I press too hard against the goat, she eats my plaits. One is already ten centimeters shorter than the other, the ribbon gone, and that makes me want to cry too.

I could stand up, but the boat is rolling and tumbling so much that I would probably fall over, and the deck is covered in water and poo and fish guts. If I don't fall over, I might bump into one of the fishermen, and they are already grumpy about having a ten-year-old on their boat. They think it is bad luck to have a child onboard. Even worse luck if she is a girl.

I could go and sit with the old man and his seasick pig, but he might ask me why I am traveling alone, all the way from Copenhagen out to the island of Bornholm, and I don't want to talk about it. That will definitely make me want to cry.

I tell myself that the goat isn't so bad. She stinks, but she is friendly, and doesn't seem to mind my being close. The softness and warmth of her remind me of snuggling by the fire with Mama, listening as she reads my favorite stories. I wrap my red woolen scarf around my head to protect my hair, rest my cheek against the goat, and close my eyes. A tear squeezes its way out from between my eyelids and dribbles down my face.

"Silly," I say, licking it off my cheek as it slides near to my mouth.

I will not feel sorry for myself.

"I will be a brave girl," I whisper into the goat's kidneys. "I will make Mama proud of me."

And then I fall asleep.

• • •

My grandmother meets me at the harbor at Svaneke. We have never met before, but I know it is her because she is the only woman there. She is short and round, like a barrel. Everything she wears is black—her headscarf, dress, boots, and shawl. Even her eyes are black, like two raisins pressed into her wrinkled gray face. She does not smile.

I wonder if her bloomers are black. Gloomy underwear would be enough to wipe the joy from anyone's face.

She waits on solid ground and makes me walk alone, down the gangplank and the full length of the long stone wharf. I have traveled all this way on my own, and still she makes me complete the final part of the journey alone.

I feel naked and lopsided, and when I reach her, I realize why.

Grandmother gasps. "What have you done to your hair, child?"

I touch my head and feel spiky tufts where one of my long blond plaits used to sit. The goat has eaten all the hair off one side of my head while I was asleep.

I can feel hot tears prickling in my eyes, but I will not let them fall. I will *not* feel sorry for myself. No matter how bald the right side of my head feels. No matter how much I wish my mother were here. No matter how long it takes before my grandmother hugs me and says that she is glad to meet me.

"Stay here, child," she says, and walks along the wharf to boss some men about. I have brought an enormous trunk with me and she is not happy. It will have to come later on the back of a cart. She will have to pay someone for their trouble.

She means *I* have caused her trouble.

I think, *Don't hold your breath waiting for a hug, Inge Maria Jensen.*

The old man walks by, leading the goat on a rope. She bleats at me. I think she is saying, "Thank you for the delicious lunch," but I am too annoyed to say, "You are welcome."

But then the man scolds her and I think that maybe the goat is feeling sad and lonely too, and I give in.

"Have a pleasant evening!" I call after her, and wave.

Grandmother rolls her eyes and drags me up the road by the arm. She will not even hold my hand.

The walk home is long and cold. By the time we reach Grandmother's farm, it is snowing, even though it is late in March and winter should be long gone. My legs are tired and my face is so raw that I don't even want to stop to build a snowman. My half-bald head stings with every new snow-flake that lands on it.

Grandmother's house is pretty. It is bright red with black beams of wood holding the red bits together. Like straw-berries and licorice. The roof is covered in a white icing of snow, but I can tell from the shape that it is made of straw thatching. This cheers me up a little. At least she doesn't live in a cave, or a hole in a tree. It happens, you know. I've read about it in fairy tales.

Inside is warm and cozy, but it is an old woman's home. There is a rocking chair by the fire, a basket of knitting, a small table with a lantern, and a Bible. There are no books full of stories and brightly colored pictures, no cat curled up by the fire, no squishy chairs big enough for two people to sit, side by side, cuddling, reading, talking, telling each other about their day.

"Well, child," Grandmother snaps. "Don't just stand there like a smoked herring with your eyes staring and your mouth open. Come inside and close the door before the wind chills the walls and there is enough snow indoors to ski."

I look up at her, thinking that she might just have made

a joke. She is frowning like an ogre. I smile anyway, and point at a flake of snow that has blown in through the door and is flitting its way toward Grandmother.

Before I know what has happened, my outstretched hand is smarting, burning, glowing red with finger shapes.

Grandmother has slapped me!

She stomps past me and slams the door shut.

"You are behaving like a barbarian, child!" she scolds. "Pointing, gaping, and disobeying your grandmother!"

I stare at her, my bottom lip trembling.

I will not cry, I say in my head. *I will not feel sorry for myself.*

But I do not know why she has slapped me. I just wanted to show her the beautiful snowflake dancing across her floor.

And I do not even know what a barbarian is.

I have never been hit before. Mama's hands were only ever used to hug, or to help with laces and buttons, or to stroke my cheek and hair.

Grandmother whips off my coat and scarf, wipes my face clean with a cold, damp cloth, and sits me down at the kitchen table with a bowl of steaming soup.

I am starving. I have not eaten since the boat left

Copenhagen yesterday. It's not easy to eat when you are watching fish guts slide around at your feet and have a sea-sick pig moaning at you. My stomach feels like it has shrunk to the size of a thimble and now it is begging for me to stretch it out with some food once again.

Grandmother says grace—"Come, Lord Jesus, be our guest. Let thy gifts to us be blest"—and nods for me to eat.

The soup looks delicious—flour balls and meatballs crowd the bowl of steaming broth, bobbing merrily between the chunks of onion and carrot.

But I am even more excited by the beautiful spoon lying beside my hand. It is large and shiny and has a pattern of flowers along its handle. It is certainly a girl spoon and perhaps even a talking spoon. There are such things. I know, because I have read about this too, in my fairy-tale book.

I lift the spoon and say, "Thank you, pretty spoon, for your help in eating my food."

Grandmother rolls her eyes and eats her soup.

I smile at the spoon and begin to eat, getting faster with every mouthful. It tastes delicious and I feel my tummy stretch and my face defrost. It is not enough, but when I have finished I say, "Thank you, Grandmother."

She looks pleased and places not one, but *three* slices of white bread before me. Then she puts a bowl of jam and a pat of butter on the table.

My mouth is watering and my tummy is growling at me to get wolfing, but I am afraid that this is some kind of trick. Perhaps Grandmother is testing me to see whether I am a greedy child as well as a barbarian.

I sit there, hands folded politely in my lap, more miserable than a goose on Christmas Eve. Grandmother is bustling around the kitchen, boiling the kettle, making tea. She is pretending to be preoccupied, but I know that she is watching out the corner of her eye.

The butter is winking at me in the light of the candle, begging me to eat it, and the jam is glistening with the goodness of a million blackberries. At last, too hungry to hold back a moment longer, I plunge my knife into the butter and spread it thickly on my soft white bread. I shovel the spoon into the jam and splat an enormous blob onto the bread, then stuff the entire slice into my mouth at once, before Grandmother can stop me.

By the time she sits down at the table with a cup of tea for herself and a glass of milk for me, I have gobbled all three pieces of bread. The remaining butter looks like it has been attacked by a hungry troll, and the jam bowl is empty except for a few blackberry seeds clinging to the sides. My cheeks are bulging with the last piece of bread and jam, my tongue is dancing with sugar, and my tummy is cheering with happiness. Only my head is filled with dread.

I look up to face Grandmother and she is nodding in approval. I cannot believe it! Her black eyes are soft and melty, and underneath the wrinkles—I gulp at the thought—her face looks just like Mama's.

"Good girl," she says. "I never could abide fussy eaters. A hearty appetite is a gift from God."

I am overwhelmed with relief. Desperate to please my grandmother, to make her love me, I smile and say, "Thank you, Grandmother. That is the most beautiful berry jam I have ever tasted."

I pick up the jam spoon and hold it to my ear.

"And the little jam spoon says it is the most delicious jam that she has ever served. She is quite giddy with the sweetness and joy of it."

It seems to do the trick, because even though Grandmother is rolling her eyes once more, her face still looks like Mama's and she doesn't slap me again this day.

• • •

I am lying awake listening to Grandmother's snoring. You'd think it would be annoying, but I am glad for it. I have never had to share a bed before, but I'm grateful that I have not been sent away into a dark corner of the house on my own. I could not bear to be all alone tonight. Not in this strange new house, so far from our apartment in Copenhagen. So far from Mama.

I think of the horrible misunderstanding with the dancing snowflake that ended with a slap and harsh words. Then I recall how pleased Grandmother seemed when I thanked her for my soup. Perhaps I should learn to be thankful for the good things as they come along, no matter how small. That would show Grandmother that I am a decent girl. It might even make her love me.

Besides, I am learning that there are many dreadful things that can push their way into my life, so I'd better enjoy the good things when I can.

I snuggle up to Grandmother, wrapping my arm around her large, soft middle. She gives an extra-loud snort all of a sudden, mumbles, "Hemph diddly diddly pom squaddle," and settles back into her deep, rhythmic snoring.

I nestle my head into her shoulder and whisper, "Thank

Thee, Lord God, that Grandmother is fat and warm and snores like a walrus with fish tangled in its teeth."

"Hork porker wallop *poomph*," Grandmother mumbles, as if she is trying to demonstrate to the Lord that she truly is a great snorer. The *poomph* at the end is so hard that I can feel the short tufts of hair rippling on my head. I pretend that it is Grandmother's special way of kissing. Like Mama used to flutter her eyelashes against mine, then press her lips against my forehead.

I stretch my face up, kiss Grandmother on the cheek, and whisper, "Amen."

Chapter 2

THE BUNNY, THE BOOK, AND THE SALTY TEARS

"Wake up, child!" Grandmother scolds, pulling the eiderdown back.

The freezing morning air turns my skin into lumpy gooseflesh. I slip out of bed and Grandmother has the sheets flattened and tucked, the eiderdown shaken, the pillows fluffed, and the quilt smoothed perfectly over the top of it all before I have fully opened my eyes.

She is standing before me like a black troll, hands on hips, frowning.

"Don't just stand there, child! There is work aplenty to be done!"

I am stripped bare, splashed with cold water, rubbed dry, and dressed in yesterday's clothes. Grandmother pulls two large woolen sweaters over my head and wraps a black scarf around my neck three times, until I almost choke. I'm sure my eyes are bulging.

She looks at my lopsided hair, shakes her head in despair, and says, "We will deal with that later. The animals are waiting."

Outside is slushy and cold from yesterday's snow, but when Grandmother opens the barn door, warm air and sweet animal smells rush at me. There are two shiny golden cows called Hilda and Blossom, a brown donkey called Levi, an enormous pig called Plenty, who is suckling fourteen pink piglets, hens and geese that don't stand still long enough to be counted accurately, and a turkey called Henry, who is as big as a tea chest.

I clomp along behind Grandmother, awkward and clumsy in the heavy wooden clogs I have been made to wear. I have never worn clogs before. In Copenhagen, I always wore leather boots, the pretty kind with pointy toes, little heels. and long silk laces. They were light and easy to skip about in. Right now, I feel like I have taken two logs, chopped a hole out of the middle of each one, and stepped in. It is true my feet are warm and dry, but I feel like I might come crashing down at any moment as I thump and limp and stumble across the barn.

Grandmother is light and loose in her clogs. I don't know how she does it.

I stop by the pigpen and smile at the piglets.

"Don't get too excited, child," Grandmother warns. "These are farm creatures, not pets. We'll be selling half in the autumn, and eating most of the others by Yule-time."

The donkey is offended. He flattens his ears against his head, pulls his lips back from his teeth, and rolls his eyes, just like Grandmother! He begins to bray so loudly and so angrily that Grandmother stomps over to where he is standing and pulls his ear.

"You cantankerous old fool, Levi!" she shouts. "You'll be the first to go come autumn-time!"

But something about the way she says it, and the way Levi swishes his tail and nibbles at her bottom, tells me that she doesn't mean a word of it.

Grandmother orders me from one end of the barn to the other, feeding, carting, scrubbing, shoveling. I muck out piles of poo so big you could disappear in them, and I almost do when I trip over my clogs and fall headlong into the donkey's stall. Grandmother makes me wash the mess off my face in the bucket of water by the door. I can still feel bits of poo in my ear, but the water is too cold to go splashing it around more than absolutely necessary.

By the time Grandmother has milked the cows and skimmed the cream off, I am exhausted and my tummy is rumbling so loudly it would scare elves out of an attic. Grandmother pours one bucket of skimmed milk into the trough and commands, "Drink up, Plenty!"

The pig grunts gently and begins to swill. *She* is not a disobedient barbarian.

I lean over the railing to her pen and whisper, "Good girl. Gobble it all up and don't forget to say thank you for the lovely meal at the end. You don't want Grandmother to slap you."

The pig looks up and snuffles her thanks.

Breakfast is bread and butter, oatmeal with fresh cream, and hot chocolate. Grandmother puts an extra slurp of cream in my chocolate, but acts as if it is nothing special.

I wait for Grandmother to say grace, then I wish the pretty spoon with the flowers on her handle good morning and dive into my oatmeal. It is the best breakfast I have

ever eaten and I think I will have to go back out to the barn
—even if it does mean clomping and slipping all the way
there and back in those big clogs—and thank the cows for
their efforts with the milk, cream, and butter. Grandmother
might think I am a naughty child, but I am not. Mama has
brought me up well.

The sudden thought of Mama for the first time this day
shocks and brings more pain than any slap could deliver. I
put my hot chocolate down and shut my eyes tight.

Don't cry, I tell myself, but big salty blobs squeeze their
way out, and before I know what is happening, my bread is
soggy. It doesn't taste nearly as good as it did five minutes
ago.

A man called Chunky Jorgensen delivers my trunk after
breakfast. I smile and say, "Thank you, Her Jorgensen," but
he doesn't even smile back at me. I wonder if I have done
something wrong once again. I look to Grandmother for
guidance, but she is too busy huffing and puffing as she
helps guide the trunk through the tiny sitting room into
her bedroom. She pays Chunky with two jars of marmalade
and a dozen eggs for his trouble, then shuts the door behind
him.

Back in the bedroom, we both stand and stare at the trunk. Grandmother's tiny cottage has a sitting room, a kitchen, and a bedroom. The bedroom has a bed, two hooks for Grandmother's clothes, and a wooden chair where she sits her teeth and her candle at night. There is no wardrobe, no chest of drawers, no blanket box for all the bits of a child's life that I have just squeezed into her home.

"Five things," she snaps. "You can choose five things to keep out, and some warm clothes. The rest must be stored in the barn."

She peels the rug off the bedroom floor, takes it outside, hangs it over the clothesline, and starts to beat the dust out.

I open the trunk and breathe in deeply. It smells like home: of Copenhagen, the parlor, my bedroom, the grass from the park across the street, the sweets from Fru Henley's Little Treat Shop, the pigeons at the windowsill, the violets that Mama used to buy every Friday to place on the mantelpiece. But most of all it smells like Mama.

I look at all the treasures inside and think that I cannot possibly decide on only five. But then I look out the window and see Grandmother beating the rug as though it has been very naughty and needs to be given the punishment of its life, and I think that I had better do as she asks.

The first thing I grab is my most precious book, *Fairy Tales* by Hans Christian Andersen. I cannot live without the Ugly Duckling, Thumbelina, and the silly Emperor. Especially not the Emperor. Whenever Mama or I felt sad, we would snuggle up together like two peas in a pod and read "The Emperor's New Clothes." The thought of that silly man walking through his kingdom wearing nothing but his bare bottom always cheered us up. Once, Mama laughed so loudly that Widow Jenkens from upstairs banged on her floor with her walking stick to make us be quiet. Bits of ceiling plaster crumbled and fell on top of us. We thought it was so funny that we laughed even louder and the widow wouldn't talk to us for three weeks afterward.

The book goes onto Grandmother's bed.

Next, I find Frederik the rabbit. He was a gift from Papa. I did not ever know my father. He drowned at sea when his ship sank somewhere between Norway and England when I was only three months old, but I am sure he was a kind man; otherwise Mama would not have married him.

Frederik's nose has been embroidered back on at least ten times, his left ear is missing, his right leg has been dipped in ink, and he has bare patches from being cuddled and loved so much. I am ten and too old for cuddly rabbits, really, but

Frederik and I have been through a lot together. He will help the nude Emperor in cheering me up.

I open Mama's enormous dictionary and look up the word *barbarian*. A barbarian is an uncivilized person, wild and rude. It sounds like a spiteful word. If Grandmother is going to call me nasty things, I really don't want to know what they mean. I throw the dictionary back into the trunk and hear a smash. I don't suppose I will be keeping the crystal vase Mama gave me for my tenth birthday, either.

Finally, I settle on my brush and mirror set (surely my hair will grow back one day!), my sketchpad and crayons, and my blue and white quilt, because it still smells of Mama.

I look out the window and see Grandmother chopping the head off one of the hens. The body is running around the backyard, blood spurting everywhere, while Grandmother stands by the chopping block, rolling her eyes. The headless hen is acting like a barbarian and wasting her precious time.

I lean back into the trunk, take one last breath of my old life, and shut the lid.

My eyes start to prickle, so I jump onto the bed with Frederik the rabbit and Hans Christian Andersen. I flick through the pages until I find "The Emperor's New Clothes," and begin to read. When we get to the part where the little boy shouts, "He hasn't got anything on! He hasn't got anything on!" Frederik and I laugh so hard that the tears roll down my face and I am feeling fine until I realize that the tears have been joined by sobs and a dreadful ache in my chest. I can't believe that Mama can feel so real all of a sudden and still be so, so far away.

Chapter 3

THE PIG AND THE PRUNES

By the end of the next day, I have learned how to muck out the stables, sweep and scrub the kitchen floor, build a fire in the hearth, make a bed, and pluck and stuff a chicken. I am not used to so much hard work. Mama and I had two servants to help in our apartment in Copenhagen. I am exhausted and Grandmother is very pleased by this.

"Idle hands make sport for the devil," she says.

I think she means that if you are exhausted from working hard all day, there is no energy left for being naughty.

It's not true, though. I still manage to be a bad girl and make Grandmother grumble like an ogre. She is not pleased when I feed Plenty the prune tart that is meant for our supper, even though Plenty had grunted and snuffled politely around my skirt, begging for food. It can't be easy looking after fourteen babies on nothing more than skimmed milk and slops.

Grandmother is even less pleased when the prunes upset Plenty's tummy.

She drags me back out to the barn, points at the brown poo dripping down the wall, and shouts, "How's *that* for Plenty?"

I try not to laugh, but I can't help it. Grandmother has made a joke, even if she doesn't know it.

I get my second slap. This time it is across the leg. I have three pairs of stockings on, so it doesn't hurt my skin, but it still hurts my feelings.

After supper, I think that I will cheer Grandmother up by reading her a story. She sits in her rocking chair by the fire, knitting balls of bright red wool. I sit at her feet.

"That's pretty," I say, pointing to the blob she is knitting.

This seems to make her glad. She doesn't smile, but nods, knits a little faster, and rocks back and forth so that her feet lift from the floor.

I open Hans Christian Andersen and read carefully

down the list of stories. I choose "The Princess and the Pea" and read in my very best storytelling voice.

It is about a prince who wants to be certain that he is marrying a real princess. His mother, the queen, places a pea under twenty mattresses and twenty feather quilts, and says that if the girl is truly a princess, she will be able to feel the pea when she sleeps on top.

I notice halfway through reading the story that Grandmother has stopped knitting. When the girl says she is black and blue all over and has barely slept a wink all night, Grandmother actually leans forward and nods. She is *excited* at the discovery that the girl is a real princess.

When I finish reading the fairy tale, I show Grandmother the beautiful colored picture in my book. The princess is trying to sleep on top of a mountain of purple, pink, blue, red, and gold mattresses, looking terribly uncomfortable, but ever so pretty.

Grandmother leans back in her chair and starts to knit again.

"Hmph!" she says. "A shameless waste of good food, if you ask me! Peas are for eating, not stuffing beneath mattresses."

• • •

The next day is Thursday. Visiting Day, Grandmother calls it. She makes me wash with extra care before I dress, and even makes sure the last bits of donkey poo are removed from my ear holes.

When we are putting on our coats and scarves, Grandmother surprises me by pulling a red woolen hat down on my head. I run to the small mirror by the door and laugh at the thick, floppy folds topped by the biggest pompom I have ever seen. This is the blob that Grandmother was knitting late into the night!

"Grandmother! It's magnificent!" I cry, and throw myself at her.

I am grateful for the amazing hat, but most of all, I am grateful that my grandmother wanted to knit it for me.

I bury my head in her chest and mumble, "Thank you! Thank you! Thank you!"

Grandmother peels me off and grumbles, "Don't fuss now! It's only a hat. Goodness knows we needed something to cover that bald head of yours."

She frowns, but we both know that I have two bonnets and a white woolen hat in my trunk out in the barn. Any one of them would hide the tufts of hair just as well, but none are as bright and cheerful as my pompom hat.

We walk along the muddy lanes side by side. At least, Grandmother walks. I slip and hobble and clomp in my wooden clogs.

I am not used to the wide-open spaces of Bornholm. There are green hills rolling over the top of one another as far as I can see. The meadows are dotted with clusters of winter-bare trees and the occasional farmhouse and barn. There is not a soul to be seen and the air is heavy with silence. In Copenhagen, there would be the rumbling of carriage wheels, the clip-clop of horses' hooves, the cries of market boys, and the chitter-chatter of people meeting in the streets.

I cannot help myself. I need to bring my own chitter-chatter to the island air.

"Grandmother," I say, "do you think a carrot would work as well as a pea?"

"Heaven help us!" she cries. "What are you prattling on about, child?"

"For the princess test," I explain. "I wonder if it has to be a pea under all those mattresses or if any old vegetable would do. A carrot, perhaps, or a bean. Maybe even a turnip."

She sighs. "A turnip would be far too big and too easy to feel."

I smile, glad that she is joining in on the fun.

"What about a small potato?" I ask.

"No, a potato would still be too large," she snaps.

"How about fruit?" I suggest. "An apple or a pear?"

"Too big, too big," she says.

"Well," I challenge her, "what about something small, like a berry? A strawberry, or a blackberry, or a gooseberry?"

I laugh because "gooseberry" is such a funny word.

She stops walking and looks thoughtful. "No, even a berry is bigger than a pea. I really think it has to be a pea. Anything else would be too silly."

She starts walking again.

"And wasteful," I add helpfully.

She looks straight ahead and does not answer, but I swear on my papa's watery grave, I see a smile twitch around the edge of her mouth!

I am too happy to talk for the rest of the journey. Besides, the mud seems to get deeper the farther we go, and I put all my energy into dragging one clog in front of the other. By the time we reach the house of Grandmother's friend, I am cold, exhausted, and starving.

Angelina Nordstrup is tall and so incredibly thin that

any hopes of a generous morning tea are dashed to pieces the moment she opens the door. Her piercing stare slips down her long nose, lands on my head, then slides all the way to my toes. She turns down the corners of her mouth and sniffs loudly.

I take my muddy clogs off and sit them to one side of the doorstep, but her disapproval still hangs in the air like a chilly fog.

"Good day and God bless you, Dizzy Bruland," she says without sounding like she means a word of it. She does not greet me.

I wonder why she is calling Grandmother "Dizzy Bruland." I know for a fact that her name is Astrid, not Dizzy. I open my mouth to explain, but Grandmother pokes me in the back.

Once we are in Angelina's kitchen, I reach up to remove my hat and Grandmother pokes me in the back again. At this rate, I will have a hole right through my body by the time we leave.

Angelina moves slowly and carefully around her little kitchen while Grandmother and I sit in silence at the table. She places teacups, plates, a tiny jug of milk, and a delicious-looking ginger cake before us. She pours tea, then cuts us each a slice of cake so thin that I can see the light through it as she passes mine to my plate. Even so, I know what good manners are and am eager to make my grandmother proud.

I smile and say, "Thank you, Angelina, for this bountiful cake."

I don't know how anyone can cut cake so finely without its disappearing into thin air, but I don't suppose Grandmother will mind the dishonesty just this once.

Then, spotting the china teapot covered in a pattern of violets, I lean forward and say, "Good day, pretty teapot, and thank *you* for pouring my tea so beautifully."

Angelina Nordstrup is staring at me as though I have just told her I was born under a toadstool and lived off slugs and worms for the first ten years of my life. Grandmother is rolling her eyes like Levi again. But no one calls me a barbarian.

I pick up my cake, carefully so that I don't tear the paper-thin slice, and it is gone in a flash. I long for more, but no matter how hungrily I stare at the cake left in the middle of the table, I am not offered another piece.

Grandmother and Angelina talk quietly about their hens, the weather, and the price of flour. There are so many silent bits in their conversation that I wonder why Grandmother has bothered to visit. There is no news about friends and family, no sharing of stories or discussion about books, no noisy games of cards or draughts, and definitely no laughter. This is the most boring morning of my life, and that includes the first morning on the boat from Copenhagen, when the captain made me sit on a barrel full of eels and threatened to throw me overboard if I made a sound or moved an inch!

By the time we leave, my bottom and legs have pins and needles from sitting still for so long and I am not sure whether I can walk home with such an empty stomach.

We are just around the corner of Angelina's stone fence when Grandmother pulls a parcel from her pocket. She unwraps the brown paper and hands me a thick wedge of cheese and an apple. I immediately forgive her for not making Angelina give me more cake.

I smile at her, shout, "Thank you, Grandmother, for this beautiful cheese and apple!," and gobble greedily.

Chapter 4

THE FLYING BUCKET

My third slap is well deserved.

I spend the afternoon in the barn with the animals. Grandmother is chopping potatoes for soup and looks so fierce with the big cleaver flying up and down that I cannot bear to watch.

I have a staring competition with the cows, Hilda and Blossom, and win. They just can't help blinking their long black eyelashes, no matter how many times I explain the game.

I sit by Plenty and her fourteen piglets and tell them the

story of "The Princess and the Pea" over and over again, trying out different vegetables. I can tell that Plenty likes "The Princess and the Pumpkin" the best, but that is probably because she would like to eat the vegetables after the princess has slept on them, and a pumpkin is the biggest of all. Greedy pig.

I argue with Levi the donkey over who can kick the hardest—him or me—and decide to solve the question with a competition. I put one of the wooden milking buckets on the floor, get a run-up, and kick it as hard as I can. I stumble in my clogs and fall flat on my face, but the bucket sails through the air and lands in the middle of the haystack. It has been a great kick! Hens and geese run everywhere, clucking, honking, and squawking. Henry appears from behind a sack of wheat and scuttles across the barn, going gobble-gobble-gobble! like one of those lady opera singers who perform at the Tivoli Gardens in summer. Levi throws his head back and brays loudly with excitement.

I climb up on the hay and retrieve the bucket. I place it behind Levi and wait.

"Come on, little donkey," I say. "Don't be shy. You can do it."

He pulls back his ears until they are sitting flat against his head, flares his nostrils, and gives a sharp kick with his back leg. The bucket doesn't fly into the air but skids across the barn floor, collecting bits of straw and string until it becomes a hairy monster scuttling after the hens.

Levi pulls his lips back from his teeth and brays like a squeaky door flapping in the wind. I can see the whites of his eyes as he rolls them around in delight.

I run for the bucket and I am so excited about our competition, I don't notice that Grandmother has slipped into the barn and is collecting eggs from the nesting boxes behind the haystack. I place the bucket in front of Levi, but before I kick, I give him a little lesson on how to get the bucket to sail high up into the air, rather than scuttle along the ground. He nods and seems to appreciate that I am trying to help him, even though this is a competition.

I push my feet farther into my clogs and stomp back to the starting position. I toss the ends of my scarf back over my shoulder, tuck my plait down inside my clothes, and look around the barn to make sure the cows and the piglets are watching. I run at the bucket, clomping like a horse, screaming like a barbarian, and kick. The bucket soars high into the air and lands, once again, in the haystack. At the same time, my clog flies off my foot and sails across the barn to the spot where Grandmother has just appeared, carrying a basket full of eggs.

The clog skims the basket, knocking it out of Grandmother's hand, and carries on past until it hits Henry in the side of the head.

Henry throws his wings in the air, cries gobble-gobble-gob—and drops to the ground with a slap.

Grandmother is looking down at a dozen broken eggs.

Levi throws back his head and laughs from the depths of his belly, braying so much and so hard that he loses his voice.

And I just stare, from Grandmother to Levi to Henry and back again. I know I must look like a herring drowning in air, opening and closing my mouth without saying a word, but I am too shocked to speak.

Finally, Grandmother steps back from the eggs. She takes one of her clogs off and tips it upside down. Three slimy orange egg yolks slip from her shoe to the ground.

I run over to see if Henry is okay, but Grandmother beats me there. She greets me with a slap across the arm and hisses, "Go and clean up that *wicked* mess, child!"

She picks up Henry's enormous body and carries it out of the barn.

I don't mind cleaning up the eggs. It's quite easy once I let Plenty out of her pen. She snuffles and licks, then sucks it all up in a blink. Grateful for the extra meal, she returns to her piglets full and happy.

I don't mind the slap either. I know that I deserved it.

But I am devastated about two things. One, that I have killed Henry. Poor fat Henry. He was just an innocent turkey going about his daily chores, not hurting anyone or expecting too much from life other than a bit of grain and the freedom to sing opera.

And two, I have made Grandmother angry. Again. I think that she will never call me Inge Maria or talk to me with a soft sound in her voice. And she will never ever learn to love me, not even just a little bit. If squashing one tiny pea is a wicked waste, what must she think of the dead turkey and the basketful of broken eggs?

It is dark when I build up enough courage to leave the barn and go back into the cottage. Henry's body is lying on a quilt in front of the sitting room fire and Grandmother is stroking his head.

"Grandmother," I say, the words tripping over the sobs that are forcing their way up my throat. "Grandmother, I am a wicked girl and I am very, very sorry. I will never do anything naughty ever again."

Grandmother sighs, and I expect that she will roll her eyes any moment now.

But she doesn't. When she looks up her face is tired, but not angry.

"No, child, you are not a wicked girl," she says. "And you most certainly *will* do naughty things again, so don't go making promises you cannot keep."

I hang my head in shame and start to cry.

Grandmother heaves herself up from the floor and walks over to where I am standing. She pulls me into the soft squishiness of her body and says, "Now then. No need to cry, child. It was only some eggs. The hens and geese will lay plenty more tomorrow, so no harm's done."

I peep out from the folds of her apron at Henry's lifeless body. I am filled with guilt and dread, but cannot bring myself to say his name. I just bury myself in Grandmother's arms and feel grateful that she does not hate me quite so deeply after all.

When I wake, it is still pitch-black outside. Someone is walking across the bedroom.

Grandmother is snoring like a walrus beside me, unaware that we have an intruder in the cottage.

I am so scared that I cannot move.

"Grandmother," I whisper.

"Hoomph piffle dordle-dordle *poomph!*" she mutters, and settles back into the steady rhythm of her snoring.

I hear the slow pit-pat pit-pat between her snores as the intruder creeps his way across the floorboards. He is coming toward our bed!

"Grandmother! Grandmother!" I gasp, now terrified. "Wake up!"

But she does not stir.

The footsteps are moving faster now. I shake Grandmother by the shoulder and tug at her hair. There is a whooshing sound and the end of the bed bumps. A terrifying noise explodes through the dark, waking Grandmother with such a fright that she sits bolt upright in bed.

Gobble-gobble-gobble-gobble-gobble!

I cannot believe my ears!

Gobble-gobble-gobble-gobble-gobble! Henry sings, joyfully, energetically, and ever so noisily.

Grandmother lights her candle and holds it up in the air.

We sit, side by side, and stare at Henry's enormous bulbous body perched on the end of the bed. His tail is fanned out in excitement, his bright red wattle dangling merrily from his beak. He tilts his head to one side, stares at Grandmother, and sings again: gobble-gobble-gobble-gobble-gobble!

"You *stupid* old bird!" she cries. "I'll be making you into a Christmas dinner nine months early if you don't keep quiet!"

But even in the candlelight, I can see that her eyes are sparkling. As I watch, her mouth turns up at the sides and she starts to shake all over like jelly wobbling on a plate.

Grandmother is laughing!

She throws back her head and laughter comes tumbling over her toothless gums. She is laughing, laughing, snorting, laughing.

Henry enjoys the joke and starts laughing too. Gobble-gobble-gobble! Gibble-gabble-gobble-gobble-gobble!

This makes Grandmother laugh even louder, and soon she has the hiccups.

I am sitting in bed with a turkey the size of a tea chest and a toothless, hiccupping grandmother. They are both laughing and tumbling around on the eiderdown and before I know it, we are all rumbling and rolling and giggling together, as happy as three peas in a pod.

"Oh, Inge Maria!" Grandmother cries, the tears streaming down her face. "I haven't—*hic*—laughed so much—*hic*—since your mama was a little girl—*hic!*"

I stare at her. Grandmother has called me Inge Maria for the first time ever, and it sounds wonderful.

I am about to tell my grandmother that I love her, but Henry scuttles up onto the pillows between us, fluffs himself up to an unbelievable size, and declares *his* love for Grandmother instead.

Gobble-gabble-gibble-gubble-gobble-gobble-gob!

Chapter 5

THE GOBBLING SONG AND
THE PERFECT PICTURE

Saturday is washing day. We build a blazing fire in the kitchen and boil pots of laundry as though we are going to make stocking soup, bed-linen stew, and bonnet broth.

I have never done laundry before. Mama always sent ours away with Dorte the maid. It would return in brown paper parcels tied up with string, clean and pressed, like magic.

It is tiring, but at least my hands are not idle and making sport for the devil. Grandmother is silent, but not cross. And now that I know she can laugh, she doesn't seem quite so scary.

When it is time to wring the water out of the bed linens, we go outside into the chilly morning air. Grabbing opposite ends of a sheet, we twist it around and around until it is a short, thick rope and nearly all of the water has been squeezed out onto the ground. The sun is starting to shine through the fog, so Grandmother declares that she will hang the washing outside for the first time this year.

I am too short to reach the line, so Grandmother goes into the barn and returns with one of the wooden milk buckets. There is an awkward moment when we both remember yesterday's disaster, but she bustles onward, turning the bucket upside down for me to stand on, and we start pegging—sheets, pillowcases, aprons, stockings, shirts, nightgowns, handkerchiefs, petticoats, and bloomers.

I stare in wonder at Grandmother's amazing white bloomers as I hold them up to the line. They are like a ship's sail, built large and billowy for catching the breeze. Even more astonishing is that they have white lace on the edges and a giant pink rose embroidered on each side at the back, exactly where her buttocks would sit.

Do not laugh at Grandmother's underwear, Inge Maria, I tell myself sternly. *You must not be bold.*

I squeeze my lips together to stop the giggles that are

welling up inside, but they must come out somehow, and soon they find their escape. A blast of squashed-giggle air shoots out my nose, and with it, a generous blob of snot. My hands have been busy, but now my idle *nose* has made sport for the devil!

I stare in horror. Grandmother's snowy white bloomers are covered in snot. It is green and thick and dribbling slowly down the leg toward the delicate lace. I try to wipe it off, but lose my balance on the bucket and fall forward. I grab the bloomers to stop myself tumbling, but end up ripping them in half before I plummet to the ground and land in the mud.

Grandmother sighs heavily and looks up to heaven as though asking God for strength. She stomps inside, stokes the fire, and puts the pot of water back on to boil for *another* load of washing.

It is early afternoon. Grandmother has finished the late load of washing and is making bread in the kitchen. I am rocking back and forth in Grandmother's chair, peeling potatoes while Henry rests his bruised head by the warmth of the fire. Turkeys do not have very big brains, so I suppose they need to be careful with the little they have.

I am excited to hear a knock at the cottage door. I'm not used to spending my time so quietly. In Copenhagen, I went to school with my friends from nine o'clock in the morning till one o'clock in the afternoon, every day except Sundays. Freja, Elsebeth, Ida, Hanne, and I were like five peas in a pod, always side by side, wrapped in a shell of giggles and chatter. Mama and I were often visiting or being visited at our apartment. There were tea parties, luncheons, picnics, concerts, dinners, and games nights. Even a walk through the park would see us stopping many times to greet and chat with friends. But here, the only people I have seen besides Grandmother are Chunky Jorgensen and Angelina Nordstrup, and they are both so quiet and lifeless that I cannot think of one nice thing to say about them. It is true that Angelina bakes a delicious ginger cake. But there is no real point in that if it is just for show, and not to be eaten.

Grandmother leaps from the kitchen all white and floury, and hisses at me to take Henry back to the barn. I understand immediately. She is embarrassed to be seen coddling a farm animal. Animals are for selling and eating. She has told me so herself.

I try to pick Henry up in my arms, but he is too big. Besides, he does not want to leave the warm sitting room.

Every time I try to put my arms around his body, he sings gobble-gobble-gobble! and slaps me in the face with his wattle.

Grandmother rushes into the room with a broom and hands it to me. She is pulling off her apron, wiping her hands, and straightening her hair. I flap the broom about and Henry gets to his feet. I sweep him into the kitchen, but just as I open the back door he sings gobble-gobble-gobble! and darts under the table, back into the sitting room.

I run after him, yelling, "Henry! Henry!"

Grandmother runs after me, hissing, "Be quiet, child!"

Henry runs around the tiny sitting room, singing gobble-gobble-gobble!, darting this way then that, winking and grinning as if this is the best day of his life.

There is an impatient knock at the front door and Grandmother looks desperate. She grabs the broom, chases Henry into the bedroom, throws the broom in after him, and slams the door shut. I run around picking up stray turkey feathers and tuck them between the pages of the Bible. Grandmother nods her approval and I glow with excitement.

"Good afternoon and God bless you, Olga Pedersen and Tina Pedersen," Grandmother says as she opens the door.

A short, thin woman with tiny glasses and a matching

gray bonnet and dress comes into the cottage. She is very old, at least one hundred and four, I think. Then, to my amazement, she comes through the door a second time and stands beside herself!

Grandmother frowns at me, but I cannot stop staring. I think she would like to pretend I am not here, but I am and my eyes are popping out of my head and my face is turning blue from holding my breath.

"Child, this is Olga Pedersen and her twin sister, Tina Pedersen," Grandmother explains.

I breathe out a sigh of relief and smile. Of course! They are twins, not one person repeating herself!

Gobble-gobble-gobble! Henry sings from the bedroom.

Grandmother's eyes fill with panic. Olga Pedersen or Tina Pedersen—I cannot tell which—says, "Goodness, Dizzy Bruland! What on earth was that?"

This is all my fault. If I had not held the kicking competition with Levi, then Henry would not have been knocked unconscious and brought inside the cottage to recover.

Gobble-gobble-gobble! Henry sings again, and I find myself mouthing the words. I make big, exaggerated shapes with my lips.

Olga and Tina stare and I burst into song:

Clap, clap, cake.
Tomorrow we shall bake.
One for Mama, one for Papa,
One for little Inge.

Olga and Tina are looking completely confused and Grandmother is shaking her head in dismay, but I soldier on.

Gobble, gobble, gobble.
Yum, yum, yum.
Gobble, gobble, gobble.
Yum, yum, yum.

I beam at Grandmother, hoping that she has noticed what I have just done. I have taken the well-known children's song and added my own verse with gobbling to cover up for Henry. I am very proud of myself.

Grandmother does not look convinced, so I start again, singing louder this time and swaying from side to side so that my single plait sways prettily.

Clap, clap, cake.
Tomorrow we shall bake.
One for Tina, one for Olga,
One for little Inge.
Gobble, gobble, gobble.
Yum, yum, yum.
Gobble, gobble, gobble.
Yum, yum, yum.

Olga and Tina look from Grandmother to me, then back again. Their gaze is filled with pity. I know they are thinking that Grandmother is in for trouble, taking this singing, swaying, half-bald child into her home.

Henry sings out from the bedroom again: gobble-gobble-gobble!

I repeat the made-up verse of my song, dancing a little jig at the same time:

Gobble, gobble, gobble.
Yum, yum, yum.
Gobble, gobble, gobble.
Yum, yum, yum.

Grandmother hustles the Pedersen twins into the kitchen and says, "Inge Maria, I think it is time for your nap."

I understand. I give her a big wink and slip into the bedroom, where I make Henry still and quiet by reading him the story of the Ugly Duckling. It is a sad tale about a duckling who is large and awkward and constantly teased for being so different from his brothers and sisters. It ends happily, though, when he sees his reflection in the lake and realizes that, over the long, harsh winter, he has grown into a beautiful white swan.

When I am finished reading, I am careful to explain that oversized turkeys with bruised brains never, *ever* turn into graceful swans. I hope that Henry isn't too disappointed.

We sit in silence for the rest of the visit. I cannot hear any talk coming from the kitchen. The Pedersen twins, it seems, are even less talkative than Angelina Nordstrup. I don't know how Grandmother can bear it!

Grandmother rocks back and forth by the fire, with Henry on her lap. He fills the entire space and still spills over the arms of the chair. She says it is so he cannot run away again when it is time for him to go back out to the barn, but I can see that she enjoys cuddling him.

I am sitting on the rug by the fireplace, drawing a picture with my crayons.

"Thank you for your help today, child," Grandmother says. "It was a difficult situation with Olga and Tina Pedersen, and you were very . . ."

Her voice trails off. She is trying to say something nice, but cannot find the right words.

"Distracting?" I suggest, looking up from my sketchbook.

"Yes," she says. "And . . . creative."

I smile.

Henry rests his head against Grandmother's neck and whispers lovingly, gobble-gubble-gibble-gobble.

"Grandmother," I say, still drawing. "Why do Angelina Nordstrup and the Pedersen twins call you Dizzy Bruland?"

She stops rocking and I can feel her frowning at me. I continue to color in the person I have drawn and wait for her to answer.

"It is just a teasing name," she explains. "Like Chunky Jorgensen. He was a very fat boy, you know. He is thin now, but everybody still calls him Chunky."

"Were you dizzy?" I ask.

She does not answer.

"Were you dizzy from spinning around too much?" I ask, pestering. "Sometimes when Mama and I went to the park we used to spin around and around in circles, our arms flying out to the sides, and then when we stopped, it was impossible to walk in a straight line. I still feel dizzy when I remember it."

Grandmother snaps, "What a foolish thing to do! Spinning around until you make yourself sick!"

But there is no anger in her face.

"Dizzy Bruland," I murmur, hoping to force the truth out of her. "Dizzy, Dizzy, Dizzy Bruland."

Grandmother sighs, rocks herself forward and stands up, her arms full of turkey.

"Heaven help me, child. You do prattle on!" she scolds, and stomps out to the barn to put Henry to bed.

When she returns, I present her with my special picture. Three fat, round figures tumble across the page, smiles stretched wide across their faces. There is a girl with a floppy red hat with a pompom the size of a turnip and a plait sticking out one side of her head. There is a turkey with three legs, but I am hoping that Grandmother won't notice this small mistake. And there is an old woman with her legs in the air, her gigantic bloomers completely exposed. The hands of the girl and the old woman and two of the turkey's feet join up so they are one big happy family, tumbling and smiling and laughing together.

Grandmother looks at the picture. She turns it upside down, then back the right way.

I shuffle nervously on my feet, waiting for a smile, a nod, a kind word.

My throat starts to hurt and I think I have offended her. Maybe the bloomers are rude. Perhaps she is annoyed that Henry has three legs. Or maybe I just can't draw well enough.

"Grandmother?" I whimper.

I step a little closer and that is when I notice. She has a tear slipping down her cheek. She brushes it aside, sniffs loudly, and says, "It is the most beautiful picture I have ever seen. I will treasure it always, Inge Maria."

Chapter 6

THE BRUTAL BATH

The next day is Sunday and apparently the Lord God expects people on Bornholm to be extra clean for His special day. We milk the cows and muck out the stables earlier than usual. Grandmother drags a big metal tub into the kitchen and fills it with water that has been heating on the fire. I remind her that we removed every last bit of donkey poo from my ears the day we visited Angelina Nordstrup, and Blossom has licked my face clean with her enormous pink tongue this very morning, but Grandmother stands over me, one hand on her hip, the other pointing to the bath.

The kitchen is chilly, even with the fire blazing and the

windows steaming up. I peel my clothes off and leap into the tub. I am just beginning to enjoy the warm, soapy water when Grandmother dunks me under as though she has been longing to drown me all week.

I come up spluttering and coughing.

"Quit your fussing, child!" she snaps.

Her fingers scratch and dig at my scalp, searching out ticks, slugs, and mice. Perhaps even rats. Whatever she is hunting, it cannot possibly escape her quick, sharp movements. I screw my face up in pain and I'm just about to yell when she dunks me under once more. This time, Grandmother holds me under for such a long time, I start to let air bubbles out of my lungs and think that, any moment now, my whole life will start flashing before my eyes. I kick and thrash until, finally, she drags me up again. Water explodes from my mouth.

Grandmother's face is dripping. She is pressing her lips together and her eyes are not looking soft or kind or patient. She blows a drop of water off the end of her nose and wipes an arm across her forehead. With a scrubbing brush in one hand and a large cake of soap in the other, she starts working at my back, my arms, my chest, my neck, washing and scouring like a madwoman. Suddenly I am falling backwards into the water as my leg is lifted into the air and scrubbed raw. I thrash and fight against her every move, but Grandmother is strong and determined and I leave the bath cleaner than I have ever been in my life. I think, perhaps, I also have less skin than ever before, but dare not say so.

The kitchen floor is sopping wet and Grandmother looks red and flustered. She bundles me in a thick towel and sends me to the fireside in the sitting room. I dress in my best clothes while she bathes herself.

Preparing for church has never been so exhausting or painful. I hope it is worth it.

It is not worth it. The walk across the hills is long and tiring, and when we arrive, it doesn't even look like a real church. It is white as a snowman, and round! Round like a barrel of pickled beets. Round like a beehive in a picture book. Round like a milking bucket or a butter churn.

I stare for a moment, mouth gaping like a salted cod, then look up at Grandmother and say, "But it is round!"

"Yes," she replies.

I screw up my nose and say, "But it is so . . . round."

Grandmother explains that some of the churches on Bornholm were built over seven hundred years ago, when there were fights and wars. The round buildings were designed to be fortresses as well as churches. They even have a row of tiny windows up high, just below the roof, for archers to lean out and shoot at the enemy.

Church is boring. There are no children other than me. In fact, the next-youngest person there is Grandmother and she is at least ninety-nine years old. She told me yesterday that she is sixty-two, but I don't believe her. There are enough wrinkles on her face to cover an elephant's bottom and her hair is as gray as a storm cloud.

The only exciting part of church is the hymns. The moment the pipe organ begins to wheeze and snuffle, the congregation springs to life. Everybody sings, but Chunky Jorgensen's wife warbles above the crowd, "Gobble-gobble-gobble-gobble."

The sound catches me by surprise and for a moment I am certain that Henry has followed us to church and is singing Tivoli Gardens turkey opera between the pews.

"Gobble-gobble-gobble-gobble," she warbles, praising the Lord God Almighty. "Gobble-gobble-gobble-gobble," on and on with such joy and such enthusiasm that I can no longer help myself. I start to hop from one foot to another and before I know what I am doing, I am singing the clap, clap, cake song:

Clap, clap, cake.
Tomorrow shall we bake.
One for Mama, one for Papa,
One for little Inge.
Gobble, gobble, gobble.
Yum, yum, yum.
Gobble, gobble, gobble.
Yum, yum, yum.

Olga and Tina Pedersen lean forward and stare at the red pompom on my hat bouncing from side to side. The priest stares down from the pulpit. Even the organist glances over his shoulder from time to time.

Grandmother pinches my ear. I do not understand why Fru Jorgensen can carry on like a turkey in full flight and I cannot, but my ear is smarting, so I stop. Everything is dull and boring once again.

The priest, Pastor Jakobsen, talks and holds his breath for long, serious stares at the ceiling until I think I will die.

He prays on and on and on and I start to daydream about bringing bows and arrows to church and starting my *own* war from the tiny windows below the roof. Finally, the prayer is brought to a close with the priest's "Amen."

I sit up straight and yell, "Amen!"

Everyone, even the organist, turns to stare at me. I smile. Grandmother must be so proud to have me here with all my best manners for everyone to see.

Chapter 7

THE UGLY MUD

At dinnertime, Grandmother makes a special announcement. Tomorrow I will be starting school in Svaneke.

At last, there will be other children for me to talk to and play with. I am excited, delighted, and scared all at once and cannot eat my supper. The yellow pea soup sits in my bowl until it is cold and clayey. Grandmother seems to understand and does not scold me for being a fussy eater.

At bedtime, she brings a candle into the bedroom and asks if I would like her to read a story.

"Oh yes, please!" I cry. I pull my Hans Christian Andersen *Fairy Tales* from under the pillow and hand it to her.

"You choose," I say, hugging Frederik the rabbit to my chest. I am bursting with suspense over which story she will read.

I have never heard "The Girl Who Trod on the Loaf," and I am ashamed to discover that the very naughty child in this tale is called Inge. Grandmother is probably worried that I will misbehave yet again in the classroom tomorrow and is reading this story as a warning. I can't say that I blame her. I think of Plenty and the prune tart, Levi and Henry and the kicking competition, and the gobble-singing in church. It is not easy to get things right all the time when you start with a new home, new neighbors, a new church, and now a new school.

I squeeze Frederik to my face. I start to sink below the eiderdown, shame sweeping through me like a cold draught, when Grandmother puts the book down on her lap.

"Hmm," she says. "I didn't remember that the girl in this story was called Inge."

I peep over the top of the eiderdown.

"She is nothing like you, Inge Maria," she declares.

I am weak with relief and snuggle up to Grandmother as she continues to read.

Inge is a poor but pretty girl who is adopted by a rich

family. One day, her new mother sends her off with a lovely loaf of bread to visit her old family, but instead of giving the bread to her poor mother to eat, Inge uses it as a stepping stone to keep her feet out of the mud!

I think of the pea under the princess's mattress and compare it to a whole loaf of bread.

"Now *that* is a wicked waste of food!" I gasp. "Especially when her poor mother was probably starving to death."

Grandmother nods and continues the tale. When Inge steps out onto the bread, it sinks and the naughty girl completely disappears, swallowed up by the mud.

"Forever?" I ask, then hold my breath with excitement.

Grandmother closes the book.

"You will have to wait until tomorrow to find out, child," she says. "It's late and you have a big day tomorrow."

I open my mouth to protest, but Grandmother has slipped the book underneath the bed, tucked the quilts around me so tightly that I can barely breathe, and blown out the candle before I can say a word.

I lie awake in the dark as Grandmother bustles in and out of the cottage, checking on the animals, latching gates and doors, stoking the fire. My head is full of pictures of naughty Inge stepping on her loaf of bread and sinking down, down, down into the mud. I imagine the mud swallowing her, filling her ears and mouth and eyes, suffocating her.

My head aches and my heart starts to thump far too hard.

Another picture comes into my mind. I don't like the picture, but I can't make it go away. It is a rainy day. I am dressed all in black and Oline, Mama's friend, is holding my hand. There is a big, long box being lowered into a hole in the ground, but I will not let myself think about what lies inside.

I can hear music floating over from Tivoli Gardens and I think of cotton candy and ice skating and magicians. Anything except what is in the box.

Oline is sobbing and the more she sobs, the harder she squeezes my hand. I start to cry because she is hurting my fingers, but I will not cry about the hole in the ground or the piles of dirt that the men are shoveling into it. I will not feel sorry for myself, because I refuse to believe that this is really happening.

I start to hum along to the music tune. I hum through the tears and the snot and the rain and the throbbing in my squashed hand.

Oline kneels down and hugs me.

"Poor child," she says. "You are overwrought with grief."

But I go on humming through the snot, because if I don't, I will want to scream. I will scream that I am not overwrought, even though I am not quite sure what it means. I will scream at the men to dig that box back up again. I will scream at Oline to stop squeezing me so hard. But, most of all, I will scream that I want my mama right now.

When Grandmother climbs into bed, I am crying.

"Grandmother." I sob. "I want my mama."

Grandmother wraps her arms gently around me. She doesn't say stupid things like, "You will be all right," or "You need to be brave and strong." She doesn't squeeze me tight and pretend that she can protect me from this horrible grief. She just lets me snuggle into her warm, squishy body and sob.

And she helps me along by weeping a little herself.

Chapter 8

GOAT GIRL AND HAPPY KLAUS

Grandmother is cross and bossy in the morning. I am made to eat *two* bowls of oatmeal and a piece of bread and jam so thick that it looks like a brick.

"You cannot learn on an empty stomach!" she says.

I think, *You cannot learn on an* EXPLODING *stomach,* but dare not say so out loud.

She fusses over every bit of my clothing and cannot be satisfied with my lopsided hair. Finally, she decides that I will just have to keep my red pompom hat on all day long, no matter how warm it is inside the classroom.

It is a long walk into Svaneke, over hills and along lanes, and Grandmother uses every minute of the way to teach me a lifetime of manners and lessons.

"Now, don't forget your 'pleases' and 'thank yous,' child, and only speak when you have been spoken to . . . The schoolmaster needs to be shown respect at all times . . . Remember to do your best handwriting. Teachers always like a fine hand. And try not to blotch the ink when you have just dipped the quill in . . . Don't go swapping your morning tea with any of the other children. I have packed you a lovely big piece of apple tart and a wedge of cheese and you will be needing every bit of it to see you through the morning and the long walk home . . . Keep your handkerchief close by. It is dreadful to hear children sniffing in class."

I smile and clomp along in my wooden clogs, saying, "Yes, Grandmother. No, Grandmother. Yes indeed, Grandmother."

When we arrive at the schoolyard, she fusses some more, straightening my hat and brushing imaginary specks of dirt off my coat. She glances nervously at the quiet girls and boys walking into the classroom.

"Remember, you are in Bornholm now, Inge Maria. This

is Svaneke Folk School, not one of your fancy Copenhagen schools where the children run wild and speak their mind as though the teacher is wrong and they are right."

I nod and try to look serious, but I am bursting to go inside.

"All right then!" she snaps. "You will be just fine, I am sure!"

She bends down, kisses me on the cheek, and stomps away down the street toward the marketplace.

I am stunned. Grandmother has never kissed me before.

She really must be nervous about my first day of school!

The classroom is crowded with children and smells like apples and mud, ink and jam, chalk and damp stockings.

I think, *This will be fun!*

A girl called Sofie says good day, drags me over to her desk, and shoves me in between herself and the wall, but does not speak again because our teacher has arrived. He is tall and serious and wears an ugly brown coat the same color as Plenty's poo.

We stand at our perfect rows of desks and say, "Good morning and God bless you, Her Nielsen."

I notice that all the girls are sitting on one side of the classroom, the boys on the other.

Her Nielsen says softly, "Good morning and God bless you, children."

We are seated and for the rest of the morning, the classroom is so quiet you could hear a duckling wink. Rustling paper, shuffling feet, and whispers behind hands are all met with a scowl. A girl sitting at the desk next to mine coughs and Her Nielsen gives her a look that would turn your heart to jelly. The girl starts to cry. I can see the tears dripping on her paper, smudging the ink. But she does not make another sound. Not even to blow her nose.

I keep my head down and work like a donkey—except that I don't pull my ears back and bray. That would be asking for trouble.

I write my spelling list ten times—although I can't see the point when I have remembered how to spell them all after the first time—and copy a chapter from my history book. My brain is about to go numb when we are told to write a story. At last, something I can really enjoy!

I write about a girl called Astrid who has a flying loaf of bread. She rides it like a magic carpet, all over Denmark, looking for children who need help to escape from wicked parents. Once she has rescued them all, she cuts the bread up into thick slices and feeds it to them with jam and cream. It is a wonderful story and I am very proud that no food has been wasted in the telling of it.

I am just writing "The end" when Her Nielsen notices that I am new to his class and asks me to come to the front of the room.

I smile at my classmates and say, "Good day. I am Inge Maria Jensen."

The children look a little surprised at my accent. I know it sounds posh here on Bornholm, but I really can't help it. We just talk differently in Copenhagen.

Her Nielsen nods his approval at my polite greeting and says, "Welcome, Inge Maria. We hope that you will be happy here and will honor your school and your parents by working hard and obeying the rules."

I gulp at the mention of my parents, but force myself to think of Grandmother, Henry, Levi, Plenty, and the cows. They are my family now, I suppose, and I will be happy to honor them.

"Yes, Her Nielsen," I say.

On the way back to my desk, I trip over my feet and

crash to the ground. Nobody makes a sound. It is dreadful. I wish they would laugh. It's what *I* want to do. But instead they put their heads down and write their stories.

A boy called Klaus helps me up and hands me my clog. He looks like he is my age. He has the dirtiest fingernails and the skinniest face I have ever seen, but he smiles and I can see from the way his blue eyes are sparkling that *he* really wants to giggle too.

The bell rings and a sea of bodies, cake, and apples spills outside. The wind is blowing a gale and noses glow, eyes water, and hats fly into the air one after the other. I grab at my red woolen hat, but I am too late. It flies off my head and tumbles across the playground.

I run after it, laughing and screaming, and it is not until I catch it at the front gate that I realize that everyone is staring at me. The short tufts of hair on my head have grown a little in the past week, but I suppose they are still quite a shock at first sight.

Sofie's eyes are popping out of her head and the other girls are starting to whisper behind their hands.

Hot tears fill my eyes, but I refuse to let them tumble free. I will not be a crybaby. Not on my first day of school.

Klaus wanders over, scratching his head.

"What happened to your hair?" he asks.

I am so embarrassed, I want the ground to swallow me up, but it doesn't. There is nothing to do but tell the truth.

"A goat ate it," I say.

I look down at my clogs and sniff.

"Really?" he asks, and when I look up his face is filled with admiration.

Three other boys move closer and all start shouting at once. Rasmus wants to tell me about the time his mother cut his hair with her carving knife because she couldn't find the scissors. Knud swears he woke up one morning to find a whole family of mice living in his hair, and when he takes his hat off I can truly believe it. His head looks like Grandmother's knitting basket before she tidied all the wool two days ago, thick orange hair tangling all over itself.

Finn interrupts, "That's nothing! I got my hair caught in the winch on my father's fishing boat last summer. Now *that* made a mess of things, I can tell you!"

He pulls his hair back off the side of his head to show three large bald patches that look like they will never grow hair again.

Klaus grins at my tufts and says, "A goat, eh?"

I nod and pull my hat back onto my head.

Her Nielsen appears, frowning.

"Inge Maria," he hisses. "What are you doing on the *boy* side of the playground?"

I stare around the schoolyard. There are seats and trees, grassed areas and cobblestones, but nothing that looks particularly suited to boys, and definitely nothing that says "No Girls Allowed Here." I do notice, though, that I am the only girl not sitting quietly on the benches by the schoolhouse.

I screw my nose up and I am about to say, "Thank you, Her Nielsen, but I think girls should be allowed to run around on the grass as much as boys."

But Klaus is standing behind Her Nielsen, doing sign language. He rolls his eyes to the side and points his thumb over his shoulder toward the girls. He shakes his head from side to side and jumps up and down. Then finally he grabs himself by the throat and starts choking. It is very realistic. His hands squeeze tighter and tighter, his eyes bulge, his tongue sticks out and lolls about, and his face turns bright red. It's a wonderful performance and I don't want it to stop, but Her Nielsen is starting to turn a little red in the face himself and I don't want to get in trouble. Especially on my first day of school.

"I am sorry, Her Nielsen," I say, with great respect and

sickly sweetness in my voice. "I will return to the girls' area straightaway."

Her Nielsen nods his approval. I head across the playground looking happy and obedient, but feeling as cross as a badger with a bee sting.

As I reach the benches, I catch sight of Klaus falling to the ground as he finally dies. He lands with a splat and his legs flail in the air. Finn, Knud, and Rasmus stagger around in grief, holding their hands to their foreheads and moaning. A fifth boy walks past and kicks Klaus in the guts, just to make sure he is truly dead.

I giggle into my apple tart.

The rest of the day is filled with music. The junior children squeeze into our classroom and Fru Ostergaard flops her fingers up and down on the piano keys as though she can barely be bothered. Her music is limp and unfeeling, but it is a relief to be able to make at least *some* noise at last.

We sing "Oh Praise Thee Lord This Happy Morn," "The Snow Is Deep O'er Hill and Dale," and "The Lark Hath Spoken to the Spring." Our voices are gentle and we stand motionless the whole time.

I long to sing the funny songs from my old school in

Copenhagen, and to dance, but nothing more jolly than a robin redbreast sitting on a twig makes its way into our melodies. What is the point of music if it sounds like an unconscious turkey is being slapped across the piano, and the words are as dull as a conversation between Grandmother and Angelina Nordstrup?

I leave school feeling sour and disappointed.

I stand at the school gate, waiting to see who is walking my way, but everyone seems to live in Svaneke or on farms along the coast. I wave at Sofie as she disappears around a hedge, push my feet farther into my heavy clogs, and set out on the long walk home.

When I come to the big oak tree at the end of the lane, I don't know whether I should turn left or right. I close my eyes and try to remember the way I walked with Grandmother this morning, but I can't. All of the hills look the same except for the one with the big red windmill, and I am certain that it's been built during the day while I was at school.

Perhaps I have been walking the wrong way all this time. I could go back into Svaneke and start again, but I truly don't think my legs can carry me that far. I plop down onto the grass, right where I am, and bury my face in my arms.

There is a tug on my plait and a voice laughs. "You're not lost already, Goat Girl?"

I look up into Klaus's skinny, smiling face.

I am ashamed of myself. I am ten and I can't even find my way home. Suddenly it is all too much to bear—the silent schoolroom, my chewed-up hair being seen by my classmates, the out-of-bounds grass in the playground, the joyless music, and now the overwhelming task of finding my way home. Big fat tears dribble down my face and I can feel my mouth going wobbly and ugly.

"Cheer up!" Klaus says, smiling. "I'll walk you home. You're almost there already."

He takes me by the hand and leads me down the laneways, over the sty, and across the paddock until we are standing at the gate to Grandmother's farm.

"Thank you, Klaus," I whisper, wiping my nose on my sleeve. They are the first words I have been able to utter, between the fear and embarrassment of being lost.

"It was nothing." He grins. "I was going past anyway."

I look at his bright blue eyes and think he is the happiest person I have met on Bornholm. Other than Henry, that is.

"Do you live near here?" I ask, hopeful that we might be able to walk to and from school together.

He shuffles and blushes.

"Sort of," he says. "Sometimes."

I am just about to ask what he means when Grandmother calls out, "Is that you, child? Come in here and help me with the piglets."

"I'd better go," Klaus says. "See you tomorrow."

I want to ask him if he will walk to school with me in the morning, but he is running like a rabbit and disappears around the bend in the lane before I can even say goodbye.

That night as we eat our supper, I say, "Did you know, Grandmother, that at my school in Copenhagen, the girls and the boys played together? The girls were allowed to run and climb and scream. Sometimes we rolled down the hills in Frederiksberg Gardens, getting grass in our hair and making ourselves giddy. Fru Hansen even rolled down with us one day. She said exercise is good for girls, and girls can do anything that boys can do."

Grandmother takes my empty soup bowl away and puts two pickled herring and a boiled egg in its place. She cuts a thick slice of rye bread and slips it under the herring.

"When we wrote a really good story at my school in Copenhagen," I tell her through mouthfuls of egg and fish, "the teacher would get us to stand before the class and read it out loud. Everyone would clap. And if it was especially good, we would be sent around to all the other classes to read it to them too."

Grandmother plops another boiled egg on my plate.

"We never got into trouble for sniffing or coughing at my school in Copenhagen," I explain. "Sometimes we were allowed to talk about our work and share our ideas, and Fru Helles liked to see us laugh. She said laughter was good for the soul. She didn't seem to think there was anything wrong with being happy."

I gulp my last piece of rye bread and wonder if I have said too much. I am determined to make Grandmother proud of me. I want her to know that I am fitting in at school, to think that I am enjoying it. Even if I'm not.

Grandmother bustles around the kitchen, piling a plate high with raisins, cinnamon biscuits, and gingerbread men. There weren't any gingerbread men living in the house this morning when I left for school. She must have baked them during the day, just for me.

I jump out of my chair and wrap myself around her fat body.

She peels me off and snaps, "Settle down and eat, child. It's only a few biscuits."

But I can tell from the twitching at the corners of her mouth that she is pleased.

I sit back down, giggle, and bite the arms and legs off one of the little men. While Grandmother makes tea, I grab two more gingerbread men and dance them back and forth across the tablecloth.

"Did you know," I say, "that at my school in Copenhagen, we used to sing every day? Fru Hansen would play the flute and Fru Helles played the piano and they sounded like a circus was coming to town. We sang happy songs and silly songs and even one that really *was* about the circus coming to town!"

I dance the gingerbread men around the table and hum "Here Come the Clowns."

Grandmother sits down with her cup of tea, narrows her eyes, and says, "You have not said anything about your *new* school, Inge Maria."

I gape at her for a moment, thinking that I have been

caught out. But I gather my wits about me, fold my hands politely on the table, and say in my sweetest, gentlest Svaneke Folk School voice, "It was very pleasant. God bless you and thank you for asking, Grandmother."

Grandmother rolls her eyes and bites the head off a gingerbread man.

At bedtime, Grandmother lights the candle and brings Hans Christian Andersen's *Fairy Tales* out from beneath my pillow.

"I think we will leave the girl who trod on the loaf of bread," she says. "It's a nasty story and I am scared that it will give me nightmares."

I smile with relief. I know grandmothers don't have nightmares. She is just thinking of me.

I tell her that I have written my *own* story about a loaf of bread at school today.

"It's a happy story," I explain, "and there is no wicked waste of food."

She listens carefully as I retell the fairy tale as accurately as I can.

"That is very impressive, Inge Maria," she says, and I feel

my chest swelling up with pride. "Far better than anything I have ever read by Hans Christian Andersen."

To prove her point, she tucks the book away under the bed and asks me to tell her another. I fall asleep halfway through my story of the fat old woman with the flying bloomers.

Chapter 9

THE BRAVE LITTLE RABBIT

School does not improve with the passing of days. I write the same spelling words so many times that I start seeing them in my sleep, and the silence of the classroom is starting to give me the fidgets. The more I try to sit still, the more my feet want to tap, my knees want to jig up and down, and my fingers want to drum on the desk. My mouth longs to make all sorts of noises it has never made before — clicks of the tongue, chomping of the teeth, deep snorts at the back of my throat and loud, blasting raspberries. I manage to control myself, but the effort is exhausting.

Worse still, morning breaks must be spent sitting on the bench with the other girls, reading and talking quietly, or playing on the small section of cobblestone between our classroom and the side fence. It is barely big enough for skipping with a rope and cannot possibly contain a game involving dragons, ogres, flying loaves of bread, and wild chases. I stare enviously at Klaus and his friends as they gallop across the grass, rolling and wrestling till their clothes are torn and their faces are smeared with dirt.

I return to the classroom, my legs still twitching and my imagination rampaging.

On Wednesday, I think we are about to have some fun when Her Nielsen announces it is time for art. I love creating pictures. But we are to draw houses and must all begin with a box and then add a roof, a door, and two windows. We may only use three colors — brown, green, and black. I long to draw big red flowers and a giraffe in the garden, but Her Nielsen says no. My house looks exactly the same as everyone else's in the end, except for Henry's face, which I have drawn peeping out of the window. It is very disappointing.

On Thursday, my heart sinks when I see Fru Ostergaard

and her twenty-eight students walk into our classroom. It is time for music again.

There is no joy in standing still while you sing, and I am bursting to move after the first four songs. I try wriggling my ears to "Come Hither Little Rabbit-O," but find it unsatisfying. When Fru Ostergaard flops her fingers over the keys for the final verse, I begin hopping a little to the words:

> *Hop, little rabbit.*
> *Hop, hop, hop.*
> *Hop, little rabbit.*
> *Hop, hop, hop.*

When the music stops, I have hopped out from behind my desk and halfway up the aisle.

Fru Ostergaard stares at me over the top of her glasses.

"What *are* you doing, Inge Maria Jensen?" she asks.

Elen Skafsgaard tugs on the back of my dress, trying to get me back to my place. But I know that Fru Ostergaard would enjoy a little dancing with her music, if only she could see how it is done. It does not need to be complicated, just fun.

I start to hop along the aisles between the desks again and burst into song:

Hop, little rabbit.
Hop, hop, hop.
Hop, little rabbit.
Hop, hop, hop.

I reach the front of the room, but still Fru Ostergaard is unimpressed. One or two of the little children are looking quite excited, though, so I think I had better keep going. The words to the rabbit song have run out, so I start to sing the first thing that enters my mind.

Gobble, gobble, gobble,
Yum, yum, yum.
Gobble, gobble, gobble,
Yum, yum, yum.

I am hopping from foot to foot, holding my hands up in front of my chest like bunny paws. Half of the junior children have joined in and we start again. After a second gobble verse, I lead a trail of little children around the room, hopping and singing:

Hop, little rabbit.
Hop, hop, hop.
Hop, little rabbit.
Hop, hop, hop.

When we get to the end, Her Nielsen is as red as a beetroot and shaking all over. Fru Ostergaard is sitting at the piano, opening and closing her mouth. I think she wants to sing, but is too overwhelmed with excitement at how fun her lesson has become.

I smile at her and return to my seat, but not before I have done a little curtsey and said, "You're welcome."

Klaus catches up to me on the way home. He is laughing and yelling before he even reaches me.

"That was spectacular today!" he cries. "I thought Fru Ostergaard was going to explode!"

"She did seem pleased with the dancing," I say.

"Pleased?'" he gasps. "She was *furious!*"

I am stunned. How could Klaus say such a thing?

"I meant to show her how fun music can be," I explain.

"Oh, it was fun all right," says Klaus. "Her Nielsen was nearly dying of laughter. I've never seen him enjoy anything at school so much."

"But Fru Ostergaard?" I ask, growing more anxious.

"She was definitely angry," Klaus says. "Steaming. Annoyed. Livid."

"What's livid?" I ask.

"Really, really cross."

I consider this for a moment, then ask, "Well, why didn't she punish me?"

"Too shocked!" Klaus laughs. "Besides, everyone else loved it. Music is horrible, but today it was hilarious."

I stop walking and kick at the mud with my clog. What will Grandmother do when she finds out? I didn't mean to be naughty, but I have disgraced myself again.

"Don't worry, Inge Maria Goat Girl." Klaus grins. "I've been talking with Finn, Rasmus, Knud, and some of the other boys, and we've agreed to dance with you next time."

"Really?" I cry.

"Really!" he shouts.

My face splits with a smile. I grab Klaus by the hand and drag him up the lane, dancing and singing:

Gobble, gobble, gobble,
Yum, yum, yum.
Gobble, gobble, gobble,
Yum, yum, yum.

Fru Ostergaard is going to *love* our next lesson.

Chapter 10

THE WICKED SCISSORS

By Friday, the "No Girls Allowed" parts of the playground are teasing and taunting me. Klaus barrels by with Knud and Rasmus. They are a pile of arms, legs, orange wooly hair, flashing smiles, and flapping green and blue scarves. I stand at the edge of the cobblestones and gaze after them longingly.

Ingrid Hansen tugs at my sleeve and says, "Don't look at those silly boys. Let's sit down and play a nice game of dominoes."

I don't know if it's the dominoes or Ingrid's quiet, gentle voice, but something snaps inside my head and I cannot bear to be a girl at Svaneke Folk School one moment longer.

I run into the classroom, pull off my red hat, grab Her Nielsen's big brass scissors, and start snipping.

First I cut off my remaining long blond plait.

Snip!

Next, I grab loose bits of hair and start cutting close to my head.

Snip! Snip! Snip!

I am stunned for a moment when I look down and see so much hair on the floor, but it is too late to go back now. I gather up the hair and throw it into the fire. I place the scissors back on Her Nielsen's desk and squash my hat into my coat pocket.

I run out the door, past the rows of girls reading books, playing draughts, and talking quietly. I race across the grass, roaring like a lion, and dive on Klaus, knocking him to the ground. I punch like a barbarian, I wrestle like a bear, and I curse like a fisherman. Finn and Rasmus join in the fun, then Knud, Ole, and Anton. I am so tangled up in the pile of boys' bodies that I am not discovered until the bell rings and it's time to go inside. Only then does Her

Nielsen notice a dress on the "No Girls Allowed" side of the playground.

I know that I am in for it.

I know that what I have done is silly and rash and probably the naughtiest thing *anyone* at Svaneke Folk School has ever dreamt of doing.

And I know that I am not one tiny bit sorry.

Her Nielsen is standing over me, trying to remain calm and understanding, but there is a vein sticking out in his forehead and his left eye is twitching. It is not the kind of twitch people get when they are trying not to laugh. It is the other kind of twitch. The one that tells me trouble is on the way.

"Inge Maria Jensen," he says, his voice soft but menacing. He is waiting for an apology.

I am surprised by what comes spilling out of my mouth, but I cannot seem to stop.

"Why do you think girls shouldn't play exciting games? And why don't you let us draw with lots of colors and fill in our page with flying camels and blue trees and three-legged turkeys? Or give us music that makes us want to dance and clap and laugh in each other's faces? Or read our stories about girls who sail to sea in a teapot and learn to talk to octopuses? Or let us cough out loud and pick our noses when they really need it?"

Her Nielsen is shuffling uneasily.

"And why," I shout, "do I have to write that stinking, rotten, pooey spelling list out TEN TIMES EVERY SINGLE DAY?"

He looks at me as though I have just gone mad. We stare at each other for a moment and the next thing that flies from my mouth takes us both even more by surprise.

"I think it's time for me to go now."

And I turn on my clogs and run.

I run.

I do not run home to Grandmother's farm. I have disgraced myself like never before and she will be ashamed of me. She is certain to smack. She might even yell or lock me in the larder.

I run down the street, between the yellow and black cottages, my short, tufty hair blowing in the wind. My stomping clogs sound rough and dangerous on the cobblestones and that is exactly how I feel. I run and run and find myself at the harbor, the place where I arrived at this horrible island less than two weeks ago.

I stop for a moment and stare longingly at the ocean. Dream of it taking me back to Copenhagen and Mama and my old life. The life where it was fun being Inge Maria Jensen.

It's no use. I am stuck here.

Angelina Nordstrup is walking down to the harbor. I cannot let her see me or she will tell Grandmother, so I run along the water's edge and duck into the first building that looks as though it might be unoccupied.

A wave of heat and smoke sweeps over me. I stumble forward, coughing and spluttering, and a bunch of dangling fish smack me in the face.

I'm in the smokehouse. Hundreds and hundreds of herring are hanging from the ceiling by their tails. The fire is loaded with sticks and it's sending out billows of thick white smoke to preserve the fish.

This should be a safe place to hide for now. Surely no one will return until the fire is dead and the wood has stopped smoking.

I huddle in the corner, grateful for the warmth. I just

wish there weren't so many bulging eyes looking down at me.

"What are you all gawking at?" I ask. "Haven't you ever seen a girl with no hair?"

The herring don't answer. They just keep on staring, their mouths half open in surprise.

Chapter 11

THE STINKING FISH

It's a very odd feeling, waking up in a smokehouse.

The first thing I notice is that my skin is hot and dry and feels too tight for my face to fit inside. The next thing I notice is the smell. These herring were stinky enough when they were fresh, but I must have been in here for hours, and now that they are shriveling in the smoke, they smell a billion times worse.

Chunky Jorgensen and another old man are leaning over me. They are both holding a handkerchief over their faces. I'm not sure if it is to stop them from breathing in the smoke or the smell of the fish. The smell is really, really horrible.

"Yes, that's her all right," says Chunky. "She's the little lass from Dizzy Bruland's farm."

The other man leans over and pokes at my cheek, then my hair.

"Doesn't look much like a girl to me," he says. "More like a smoked herring . . . or a smoked pig."

Klaus pushes his way in between the two men and grins at me.

"Eww! You stink, Goat Girl!"

He waves his hand back and forth in front of his nose and begins to laugh.

"You don't look too good, either," he says. "Come on. I'll take you home."

I don't want to go home, but I don't see what else I can do. I can't stay here with the herring now that I've been discovered.

Chunky and his friend step aside while Klaus drags me out of the smokehouse. Chunky shouts after us, "And don't you go stealing any fish on the way out, lad! I'm awake to your capers, never you mind!"

I am about to ask Klaus what Chunky means, but I am too shocked by how dark and chilly it is when I step outside. It is terribly late. I must have been asleep for hours and hours, probably smoked into a daze.

I stop at a water pump and drink like a camel. When I feel more like a girl than a dried-out fish carcass, I stand up straight and stare at Klaus.

"What are you doing here, anyway?" I ask him. "Shouldn't you be home, in bed?"

Klaus looks suddenly embarrassed, but then smiles his dopey, friendly grin.

"Shouldn't *you?*" he says.

I wipe off the water that's dribbling down my smoky, dried chin.

"That's different," I say. "I'm running away from home."

"You *were* running away from home," Klaus corrects me, and he takes my hand and drags me away from the smokehouse.

We are still walking along the harbor when a cat joins us. It leaps down from a stone fence and meows noisily. I am too tired to stop and stroke it, but it follows us anyway. Klaus sniggers a little, but I don't see what's so funny. It's just an ordinary black and white cat.

Once we have turned the corner and are walking up

the hill, two more cats join us—a big ginger tomcat and a pretty little gray one. There is a full moon tonight and I think that perhaps the cats are heading out to some sort of gathering on the hills.

By the time we are passing the school, there is a whole crowd of cats trailing behind us, mewing and trotting along with their tails in the air. Klaus is now laughing uncontrollably and I am getting cross.

I stop and turn toward him, my hands on my hips. The cats start meowing more than ever and jostle with one another to weave in and out of my legs. I am caught in a sea of smooching, purring fur.

"Why are you laughing?" I yell.

A black kitten is climbing up my skirt. I peel it off and hold it in front of my face.

"And why are all these cats following us?" I cry.

"Not us!" Klaus says. *"You."*

And then he is laughing so much that he needs to lean against a tree for a moment to stop himself from tumbling over.

I don't understand.

"All these cats are following *you*," he explains. "You stink!"

I lift my arm and sniff. I do smell a *bit* fishy, but not as bad as the inside of the smokehouse just before I left.

"Trust me," Klaus says, grinning. "You smell like a fishing boat that's just come in from sea. *You* can't tell because you have been surrounded by it. You've grown used to the stench."

The kitten licks my nose.

"You really, *really* stink," he says, "and the cats love it."

I moan and put the kitten on the ground. We walk on up the lane, my skin tight and dry, my hair short and tufty, twenty-seven cats at my heel and a skinny blond boy at my side who cannot stop laughing no matter how many times I hit him.

By the time we reach Grandmother's farm, Klaus's wild laughter has settled down to giggling and the occasional snort. He's carrying the black kitten and there are now only eight cats still with us. The rest have gone home, tired of waiting for the fish dinner that we have not shared.

Klaus tucks the kitten into the pocket on my skirt and says, "I'd better go."

He has run off down the lane before I have even said thank you. Gone in the opposite direction from the way he ran on Monday. I wonder where he could be going at this time of night.

I walk toward the house, the cats tangling in my legs with every step.

"Shoo!" I say. "Go on home."

But I'm exhausted and they know my heart's not in it, so they stay.

The front door flies open and Grandmother's worried voice shouts, "Inge Maria, is that you?"

I step into the light of the sitting room and Grandmother gasps. She does not know where to look first—at my hair sticking up in short, dirty clumps all over my head; at my face, which is smoked, wrinkled, and brown like old leather; at my clothes, which look like they have been pulled from a bonfire; at the tiny black mountain climber who is scaling my body; or at the eight cats who are now howling as they rub around my legs, waiting for the fish that they believe I have tucked away somewhere inside my clothes.

Suddenly, she steps backwards as though she has been belted in the head with a frying pan, and covers her nose with her hand.

"Inge Maria Jensen! What *have* you done?" she cries.

And before she is even expecting a reply, the whole story

comes tumbling out—about the horrible stillness of the classroom that makes my legs twitch and my mouth bubble and froth, the injustice of a schoolyard where only boys are allowed to roar and tumble and gallop and the girls are not considered worthy of the grassed areas and, finally, the incident that started with the big brass scissors and ended with me being smoked like a herring down by the harbor.

The kitten is now perched on my shoulder, licking the inside of my ear, and the cats are howling in sympathy with my own howling and sobbing.

Grandmother mutters angrily and shakes her head. She grabs the broom and sweeps the cats, one by one, out the door.

When she turns to look at me, she sighs.

"For goodness sake, child! You smell like a bucketful of rotting prawns. It's only Friday and already I need to get the bath out."

She storms into the kitchen, yelling over her shoulder, "That smell is going to stick with you for days, maybe weeks, and school won't want you back until it's gone."

My heart skips with joy at her words.

"I'm too old and too busy to be playing teacher to a ten-year-old girl, but it will have to be done," she grumbles on.

"And don't think I haven't noticed that black fleabag you're carrying around with you!"

I follow her into the kitchen, where she grabs the kitten and shoves his face into a saucer of cream. Cream! For a little stray!

Grandmother grumps and stomps around like the weight of the world is on her shoulders. But she does not fool me for one minute. She likes the fleabag and she is glad that I will be home with her again for a week or two.

Chapter 12

A LESSON IN MANNERS

It is Saturday morning. It's still dark outside and my fingers are aching, but I'm as happy as a hedgehog in a pile of leaf litter. My head is resting against Blossom's side and I'm tugging on her teats. I can hear the hay digesting in her belly and it makes warm squelches that sound like music. I hum along:

Gobble, gobble, gobble.
Squelch, squelch, squelch.
Gobble, gobble, gobble.
Squelch, squelch, squelch.

Grandmother has filled her bucket with Hilda's milk in the time it has taken me to cover the bottom of my bucket, but I'm starting to get the feel of it. Blossom has been very patient. She only kicks when I squeeze too hard, and even then she is careful not to kick the same spot on my shin twice.

Fleabag is running around on the straw nearby, chasing bits of twine, until Henry trundles out from behind the haystack and catches his eye. Fleabag crouches down like a tiger, ready to hunt. As Henry approaches, the kitten's bottom goes up in the air and wriggles from side to side, but his head and shoulders stay low. He thinks Henry has not noticed him.

Fleabag starts to creep, slowly, softly, circling around behind the enormous turkey. He breaks into a gallop, then sprints at Henry. His little legs are just bending for the final leap of the hunt when Henry fluffs up his feathers and sings: gabble-gibble-gubble-gobble-gobble!

Fleabag leaps into the air, eyes popping out of his head with terror, back arching, fur puffing up all over. He lands at Henry's feet, hisses, and flees behind a sack of wheat.

Henry flaps his wings and laughs. Gabble-gobble-gibble-gobble!

Levi pulls his ears back, rolls his eyes, and brays in delight. Plenty's piglets start to squeal.

Grandmother grumbles, "Be quiet, the lot of you, or I'll turn you into sausages."

But no one takes any notice. We see her giving Fleabag the first of the cows' cream while it is still warm, even though she hides it behind the nesting boxes. And that carrot Levi is munching didn't just appear from thin air.

When our chores are done and I have eaten a big bowl of oatmeal and two slices of bread and cheese, Grandmother slaps a pile of paper and a pencil onto the kitchen table. It is time for my lessons.

I sit up straight and fold my hands, waiting for instruction. More than anything, I want to show Grandmother that I can be a good student, despite my disappointing start at Svaneke Folk School.

"Your duties this morning are these, child," she says as she boils the water for the laundry. "One, you will write a story that contains a bowl of oatmeal, a fox, and a black kitten."

I beam at her and clap my hands for joy.

"Two," she says, "you will write out the recipe for gingerbread men, doubling the ingredients. We will then bake them to take on our visit to the Pedersen twins this afternoon."

I am excited that I will learn to bake, but almost wish I were back at school so that I did not have to visit deadly dull Olga and Tina.

"And three," she says, cracking a wooden spoon down on the table so that I jump with fright, "you will write a letter of apology to Her Nielsen for speaking with disrespect and running away from school."

I didn't see *that* coming. I open my mouth to protest, but Grandmother is standing with her hands on her hips, glaring, daring me to argue. I hate the idea of apologizing, but deep down inside I know that Grandmother is right. Mama would have done the same. It is okay for me to disagree with my teachers. Okay even to challenge the rules that I think unfair. But it is not okay to do it in a way that is rude and disrespectful.

I take a sheet of paper, pick up the pencil, and start with the letter:

Dear Her Nielsen,
It is with my deepest apologies that
I write to say that I am sorry and filled

with remorse. Please excuse me for being disobedient and disrespectful and rude and bold and naughty on Friday. I should not have used your scissors without asking. I should not have spoken to you with anger in my voice and eyes. I should not have run away without saying "Please, may I be excused?"

I would like to take this opportunity to address my grievances in a polite and mature manner so that I am not tempted to yell at you again when I return to school.

First, girls are not idiots or weaklings. Girls can do anything boys can do and sometimes they can even do it better. I reckon Elen Skafsgaard could outrun any boy at our school if she was just given the chance, and my grandmother can milk a cow faster than you could even dream of doing it. Please give the girls at our school the chance to run and play on the grass. Maybe you could even let us yell every now and then—perhaps every second Monday.

Second, stories and paintings are the windows to a person's soul. If we make all our pictures the same, I am scared that we will lose the bits of us that make us sparkly and happy and unique. And shouldn't we share the beautiful stories we write? Imagine how sad it would be for us all if Hans Christian Andersen's teacher had forbidden him to share his fairy tales about mermaids, talking teapots, and flying suitcases!

Third, do you think Fru Ostergaard is really the best person to teach us music? I do not.

Last of all, that brown coat you wear every day is ugly and is probably the reason why you feel so grumpy all the time.

Yours sincerely,
Inge Maria Jensen

Chapter 13

VIGGO AND THE EGG THIEF

I am carrying two baskets as I hobble along the lane in my clogs. One is full of gingerbread men. The other is lined with Grandmother's torn bloomers to form a cozy bed for Fleabag, who is curled up, fast asleep. Grandmother said we could not leave him at home or he might scratch the furniture and make a mess on the rugs, but really it is because she loves him and can't bear to leave him behind.

We are barely over the top of the first hill when a white cat joins us. It is meowing excitedly and is soon joined by a gray and white cat and a big black tomcat. I don't suppose

Grandmother's ferocious scrubbing, or all that lavender oil she poured into my bath, has made much difference to the smell of me yet.

As we approach the Pedersens' farm, a large gray dog appears from nowhere and chases the cats across the fields. Grandmother sighs with relief.

Tina and Olga's cottage is the prettiest home I have ever seen. It is bright yellow with black trimmings and a newly thatched roof. The garden is full of early spring bulbs and there is a little wishing well out front that looks like it really might be magic. By the time we reach the front gate, the dog has returned to greet us, woofing and wagging his tail so hard that the back half of his body wags back and forth with it.

"Quiet! Sit down, Viggo!" snaps Grandmother. Viggo stops barking and sits down!

Fleabag has woken and is peering over the top of his basket. Viggo whines. He obviously wants to bark at the kitten, but Grandmother has told him to hush and he is too scared to disobey.

I pat Viggo on the head and he raises his paw. I shake his hand and say, "Hello, Viggo. I am very pleased to meet you."

Fleabag leans over the edge of his basket and swipes his claws across Viggo's ear. The poor dog collapses to the ground, yelping in agony, while Fleabag hisses and crawls his way up onto my shoulder. The tiny sharp claws give me a fright and I drop the basket of gingerbread men.

Olga and Tina Pedersen come out to greet us and find Viggo rolling around, howling, squashing all the snowdrops and jonquils in their garden beds. I am on my knees, brushing bits of grass and dirt off the gingerbread men as I pop them back into the basket. Grandmother is holding Fleabag up in the air and shouting, "Good day and God bless you, Tina Pedersen and Olga Pedersen!" while pretending that everything is normal.

"Good day and God bless you, Dizzy Bruland," they say together, then, "Good day and God bless you, Inge Maria Jensen."

It is the first time anyone on Bornholm has bothered to greet me properly! I look up at them and flash my brightest smile. I hold a muddy gingerbread man in the air and jig him about. I am astonished to see both little old ladies smile brightly in return.

"Come in! Come in!" cries Olga — or maybe it is Tina. I can't tell them apart.

We are hustled inside, and before Grandmother can stop them, they have removed my coat and my big red woolen hat. My hands fly to my head to cover the short, messy tufts of hair, but Tina (or maybe Olga) just chuckles like a bantam hen and says, "Oh deary, deary me. Then it's true about the scissors."

Olga's (or maybe Tina's) nose twitches, her eyes boggle, and she clucks merrily, "*And* the story about the smokehouse! What a smell!"

The twins each grab one of my arms and walk me through to the kitchen, chattering and rubbing my tufty hair. I realize, with a mix of delight and confusion, that it is my naughtiness that has made them so chirpy and excited.

They sit me down and fill my glass with milk and my plate with apricot Danishes, then bombard me with questions. They have heard the story secondhand from their neighbor, who ran into Chunky Jorgensen's friend Ulrik this morning while buying smoked herring down at the harbor. Now they want to know every little detail and I can't say I blame them. Their lives seem so quiet and boring that I'm sure a story about a wild and wicked girl cutting her hair, wrestling with the boys, scolding her teacher, hiding out in the smokehouse, and running through the town, smelling like a giant rotten herring, with dozens of cats trailing behind, would bring them much joy. But I look from Grandmother to the Pedersen twins and say the only thing that I can:

"I was a very naughty girl and I am sorry for all I have done."

Grandmother nods in approval.

I lean over toward the blue and white striped milk jug and say, "Good day, pretty jug. Thank you for sharing your milk with me."

When I look up, Grandmother is sighing and the twins are chuckling again. I bite into an apricot Danish.

Tina and Olga are impressed by our gingerbread men and don't seem to notice that some of them have two heads or just one leg. They don't even mind the dirt and grass that is still sticking to them. They nibble and smile and continue to feed me pastries until I am certain I will burst.

Finally Grandmother says, "You may be excused, Inge Maria. Why don't you go outside for a play with Viggo? I will look after Fleabag."

I slip two gingerbread men into my pocket and go out

into the garden. Viggo greets me cautiously, then frolics with joy when he is certain that Fleabag is not with me. We run up and down the laneway in front of the cottage. I scream as I feel the cold wind blasting through my shaggy tufts of hair, and laugh as my clogs splash through the mud.

There is a sudden ruckus coming from Olga and Tina's barn, at the back of their house. Viggo's ears prick up and he lets out a low growl. We both run around the back to investigate.

I freeze in my tracks. I cannot believe what I see.

Viggo has frozen too. His hackles are up all along his back and he is snarling, baring his sharp white teeth.

"Sit down and be quiet, Viggo!" I command, and am surprised that he obeys. I pat him on the head and tell him he's a good boy.

Then I glare angrily at Klaus, who is standing at the door to the barn, his sweater bunched up to form a pouch for ten big brown eggs. We have caught him red-handed, stealing.

Klaus is blushing from the collar of his shirt right up to the roots of his hair. He tries to smile, but his mouth turns up for a moment, then down, and his bottom lip begins to tremble.

My anger disappears and I am left feeling sorry for him. I know better than anyone what it feels like to be caught in the middle of naughtiness.

I hurry over to Klaus and whisper, "What on *earth* are you doing?"

He looks down at his worn clogs.

"Stealing eggs," he mumbles.

"I know *that*," I say, rolling my eyes like I have seen Grandmother and Levi do so many times. "But why?"

"You wouldn't understand," he says.

"Yes, I would!" I retort, offended. "I am a very smart girl, even though Her Nielsen doesn't believe it."

Viggo moves forward, snarling softly as he senses my anger.

"Sit down and be quiet, Viggo!" I snap. He sits again and wags his tail in the dirt to apologize.

I feed Viggo a gingerbread man and cannot help noticing how hungrily Klaus stares. I pull the other gingerbread man out of my pocket, hesitate, then offer it to Klaus. He shoves it in his mouth all at once and Viggo whimpers softly as he sees his second treat disappear.

I look at the eggs, then over toward Olga and Tina's

house, then back to Klaus's face. Stealing is wrong and Klaus knows it.

"Why?" I ask again.

He doesn't answer.

I grow cross and snap, "What would your mother say if she knew?"

Klaus's face is flooded with a look of such longing and emptiness that I regret my words immediately. I know what that look means. I have worn it on my own face many times in the past few weeks.

Klaus's hands drop to his side and the eggs fall to the ground, smashing.

"Inge Maria!" Grandmother calls from the front of the house. "Inge Maria, it is time to go home."

"Quick! Run!" I say, and shove Klaus away. He darts behind the barn and heads off across the back paddock. I don't know where he is going, but at least he will not get caught stealing. Not today anyway.

I take one last look at the slimy mess of eggs and dirt, then run around to the front garden, Viggo barking and snapping at my heels. Grandmother has Fleabag and my coat and hat in her hands. She is thanking and farewelling Tina and Olga.

I am halfway through the front gate when I turn around and say, "I have done a very naughty thing."

Grandmother stops in her tracks. I immediately regret my words, but it is too late. I must make the best of what I have begun.

"I collected the eggs in the barn for you," I stammer, making the story up as I go along. "But when I got to the door, I tripped on my clogs and dropped them all."

Grandmother looks at Tina and Olga and rolls her eyes so hard that she goes cross-eyed.

"They are all *completely* ruined," I say, then add, "I am quite ashamed of my destructive, ungrateful behavior and hope that you will find it in your kind hearts to forgive me someday."

I wait for Tina and Olga to gasp, to put their hands on their hips, or at least say, "Tut-tut!" But their eyes sparkle and Tina (or maybe it is Olga) lets a little chuckle slip before I have walked through the gate.

We are just starting along the lane when I hear one of the Pedersen twins say, "What a girl! She is as spirited and jolly as Dizzy Bruland describes her."

"Oh yes!" replies the other. "Dizzy Bruland must feel blessed to have such a child in her life!"

For a moment I think I have heard incorrectly. Perhaps she said, "Dizzy Bruland must feel *distressed* to have such a child in her life."

I glance guiltily at Grandmother, but instead of frowns and storm clouds, I see a twinkle in her eye, a smile being forced away from her lips, and a look on her face that cannot be mistaken for anything other than pride.

This *can't* be because of me.

Can it?

That night, as Grandmother snores beside me and Fleabag licks Frederik the rabbit's face, I think of Klaus. I think about his friendly smile and kindness toward me, and I know that deep down inside he is a good boy. He wants to be a good boy just as I want to be a good girl.

Fleabag bites down on my earlobe and I let out a yelp.

Grandmother stirs.

"Snork porkle hoddle poggle *poomf*," she mumbles and rolls over onto her side. The eiderdown moves and Fleabag pounces, first on one spot, then another, until he is convinced that he has all the bedding under control. He stalks around like a tiger, then curls up on Grandmother's pillow, tucked under her chin. The moonlight is shining through the bedroom window and I can see Fleabag's fur rippling as Grandmother snores great blasts of air out her nose and mouth. He purrs and falls asleep.

Klaus's smiley face drifts back into my mind. I see him tumbling across the playground with Finn, Knud, and Rasmus. I feel the welcome touch of his bony hand taking mine as he leads me home when I am lost after my first day of school. I hear his giggles as the cats follow me home from the smokehouse.

But suddenly, I see him with his sweater full of eggs outside Tina and Olga Pedersen's barn, and I recall Chunky Jorgensen's words at the smokehouse about stealing the fish, and I know.

Klaus is a thief.

I do not want to believe it, but I already know it is true.

And I am filled with a new kind of sadness and dread that I have never felt before.

Chapter 14

THE GREEDY GIRL AND
THE CAKE MIRACLE

It is Sunday and I am dunked in the bath water time after time after time. A whole cake of soap disappears as Grandmother rubs and scrubs me mercilessly, and I am scared that if she sticks that cloth any farther down my right ear hole, it will come out the left.

"You still stink of fish, Inge Maria!" she cries, and as if to prove her point, a ginger cat springs onto the windowsill and rubs against the glass, meowing to be let in.

Grandmother tips three more splashes of lavender oil into the bath and tells me to soak until she returns from feeding Plenty her slops.

It doesn't work.

On the way to church we are joined by a black and white mother cat, her five half-grown kittens, and an enormous ginger tomcat. Grandmother tries to get rid of them before we reach the church, but they will not go away. Luckily there is a heavy wooden door that is enough to keep even the hungriest cats at bay during the service.

Tina and Olga Pedersen wave us into their pew so that I am sitting between the two of them. They smile and pat my red woolen hat, cluck like two mother hens, and only screw their noses up once or twice at the smell of me. Tina (or maybe it is Olga) slips me a little bag of almond biscuits before the service begins. They do not even scowl at me when I try to sing the first hymn with my mouth full and spit crumbs all over the back of Angelina Nordstrup's black coat.

When Chunky Jorgensen's wife breaks into song like a turkey full of joy, I am careful not to get carried away. I sing the words exactly as they are written in my hymn book and only allow myself to hop gently from one foot to the other. I cannot be sure, but I almost think Grandmother is disappointed that I have not created some new sort of song to worship the Lord with this day. I make up for it by shouting "Amen!" at the top of my voice at the end of every prayer and a few other times in between for good measure. Not only does this seem to keep Grandmother more alert through the sermon, it seems to keep Tina and Olga happy as well.

As we are leaving the church, Angelina Nordstrup asks Grandmother and me to tea tomorrow. She makes a special point of telling me that she will make her ginger cake again. As if there is some great fun in seeing how thinly she can cut her delicious cake!

As Angelina turns to walk away, I say sweetly, "Excuse me, Angelina Nordstrup, you have a little something stuck to the back of your beautiful coat."

I step forward to brush the biscuit crumbs off that I have splattered there during the hymn.

Angelina gives me a smile that is almost as thin as her slices of ginger cake and says, "Why thank you, child. That is very helpful of you."

One of the Pedersen twins covers her nose and mouth with her handkerchief. The other turns quite red and makes an odd snuffling noise. I wonder if Tina and Olga both have colds or if they are, in fact, sniggering at what I have just done.

Grandmother is frowning at me like an ogre.

I am snuggled up in bed, staring at a picture in my fairy-tale book. A clock, a walking stick, and two cushions are holding a lively discussion.

"Grandmother," I say, "do you believe that teapots and spoons and spinning tops and dolls can talk?"

Grandmother stops halfway through hanging up her clothes and considers my question for a moment. I am scared in case she says no, but I think it is an important thing to know. Hans Christian Andersen says they do.

She declares, "I think that there are many things of which we cannot be certain."

She picks Fleabag up from the floor and plonks him in the middle of the bed.

"Of course, I have never heard my own teapot talking," she says, "and I am quite sure that my dolls didn't ever speak to me when I was a girl."

Grandmother climbs into bed and continues, "But that does not mean that they were not *able* to talk. Perhaps they just *chose* not to talk. After all, what would a teapot have to say to me? 'Ouch, that water is far too hot!' or 'For goodness sake, will you please empty these old soggy tea leaves out of me before I catch my death of cold?'"

"Your doll, though, might have something important to say," I suggest, "like 'Could I please wear the pink ribbon in my hair today instead of the cream ribbon?' or 'When is that handsome tin soldier coming to visit again?'"

Grandmother laughs at the idea and says, "My poor doll would have been more likely to say, 'Can you please get me out of this cupboard to play once in a while?' I was a very rough little girl and didn't much like to play with dolls. I thought it was far more fun to run and climb trees and play chases with the boys."

"Like me!" I cry, delighted at the idea.

"Yes, child. Like you."

I throw my arms around Grandmother's wide, squishy middle and say, "I love you, Grandmother."

"Now now, child. Let's not get carried away," she mutters, but I know by the soft look in her eyes that she is glad for my words.

"Let's see," she says, opening my fairy-tale book. "How about 'The Emperor's New Clothes'?"

I feel suddenly cold and sick. I cannot bear the thought of reading this tale. The Emperor is someone who marched his silly, bare-bottomed way through story times with Mama. I have tried to read him only once without her, when I first arrived on Bornholm, and it was not a happy moment.

"I'm tired, Grandmother," I whisper. "Can I please go to sleep now?"

I pull the eiderdown over my head and disappear into the dark with Frederik the rabbit and a yucky, empty feeling growing where the love and joy have just been. I wonder if these ugly moments will ever go away. If the longing for Mama will ever stop hurting so much.

Angelina Nordstrup barrels out of her cottage to greet us. She does not stop to screw her nose up at my rotten-fish odor or the three cats that have joined us along our way. She does not even remember to greet us with a blessing.

She shouts, "Oh, Dizzy! Inge Maria! Such dreadful, dreadful news!"

She looks so excited and so terribly pleased that I cannot believe that anything bad has really happened. She drags us inside and shoves us through to the kitchen, where she already has a pot of tea and a ginger cake on the table.

"You will never guess what has come about!" she cries. "So very, very frightful!"

She cuts three thick slices of ginger cake and just about throws them onto our plates so that she can get on with her tale. I barely have time to gasp, "Thank you, Angelina, for this bountiful *slab* of cake!" before she is prattling.

"There is a thief in the neighborhood! Fru Tomlinsen called in this morning to warn me that her larder had been raided overnight. Five jars of her best preserves have vanished into thin air, and there were crumbs all over the kitchen floor where the thief had gobbled an entire loaf of bread right there on the spot. The nerve of him!"

Grandmother raises her eyebrows and looks surprised, although I'm not sure whether it is because of the theft or the generous slices of cake that Angelina has just served us.

I am astonished at both. I know immediately who the thief is, but concentrate on scoffing my cake before it is taken away.

"And so," Angelina says, babbling, "I thought I had better check my larder just in case there has been any mischief afoot in my own home, and what do you think I found?"

Grandmother sips her tea and stares at Angelina, but

will not guess. I think she is too stunned by how interesting this visit has suddenly become. Especially at how lively Angelina Nordstrup has become. It is nothing less than a fairy-tale miracle.

Angelina cuts me a *second* large slice of ginger cake and cries, "*Three* jars of gooseberry jam and a *whole* wheel of cheese were gone!"

She sits back in her chair, folds her arms, and nods rapidly.

"Oh dear," says Grandmother, although once again, I am uncertain as to whether she is reacting to Angelina's tale or the sight of me shoveling a second slice of cake into my mouth all at once. I smile through the crumbs and lemon icing and mutter "Thank you" again, just so she knows that I am grateful for this sudden bounty.

I swallow and say in my sweetest voice, "Please, may I have some more cake?" I cannot believe that I will ever get the chance to eat so much of Angelina Nordstrup's delicious baking ever again.

She has completely lost her head in the excitement and serves me yet *another* slice! I ignore Grandmother's scowl and concentrate on eating as I hum the tune of "Come Hither Little Rabbit-O."

Angelina sips her tea and nibbles her own slice of cake, full of nerves and joy.

"Who do you think would do such a dreadful thing?" she cries.

I think of skinny Klaus, the stolen eggs, and the way he scoffed Viggo's gingerbread man.

"Someone hungry?" Grandmother asks.

"No, no, no, no!" cries Angelina. "It is certain to be someone truly wicked."

Grandmother sips her tea quietly while Angelina prattles on.

"Chunky Jorgensen and Her Tomlinsen have decided to gather a night watch. A group of men will patrol our farms at night. I suppose they'll be carrying pitchforks to defend themselves against the villain. They might even take dogs. When they catch the thief, as they most certainly will, he will be handed over to the police and locked away in prison where he belongs!"

A horrible picture of Klaus being poked by pitchforks and chewed to bits by vicious dogs rushes into my mind.

I gulp.

Angelina and Grandmother stare at me.

"I'm sorry," I say. "I think I have a lump of cake caught in my throat."

As we walk home, I am uncertain whether the sick feeling in my tummy is from eating half a ginger cake in less than ten minutes, or from fear at the thought of Klaus being caught and thrown into prison for the rest of his life.

"Grandmother?" I say, burping. "Can children be thrown into prison?"

Grandmother peers at me out of the corner of her eye.

She asks, "Do you know something about the stolen food, Inge Maria?"

I peer back at her out of the corner of *my* eye and decide that I should probably change the topic.

"Do you think Fleabag will have piddled on the rug when we get home?" I ask cheerily.

Grandmother sighs and rolls her eyes like Levi.

When we get home, Fleabag *has* piddled on the rug. I am glad because it distracts Grandmother, and she does not think to ask about the thefts again.

Chapter 15

THE WINGED APPLE TART

After I have bathed again on Tuesday morning, Grand-mother declares that I smell no worse than a pot of boiled cod. I should be able to return to school the following Monday.

Grandmother quizzes me on twenty of the trickiest spelling words she can think of and seems quite disappointed that she cannot stump me. I know how to spell every single one. I write a story about an owl, a dictionary, and five china teacups, then write out the recipe for apple tart, tripling the ingredients.

We each bring an armful of apples in from the barrel in the barn and spend the rest of the morning stewing fruit and baking three enormous apple tarts. Grandmother puts two away in the larder and sets the third outside on the kitchen windowsill to cool so that it will be ready for our afternoon tea.

We walk across the hills and past the church to the priest's house to deliver three dozen eggs, and not a single cat joins us. I am very proud of myself and my almost clean skin.

When we get home, Grandmother asks me to return the egg basket to the barn while she pops the milk on the stove for my hot chocolate. I run through the garden singing "Here Come the Clowns." I half dance, half skip around the corner of the house and crash headlong into Klaus. I scream in surprise! Our apple tart flies from Klaus's hands into the air. Klaus falls backwards into the mud, where the tart plops beside him and I land on top of him with a grunt.

Grandmother rushes out the kitchen door to see what all the noise is about. She stands with her hands on her hips, scowling.

I pull myself off Klaus and stand up.

"Grandmother!" I gasp.

I rack my brain for an explanation that will hide the fact that Klaus is Bornholm's wicked thief.

I stare at Klaus and the splattered tart. The beautiful blue and white pie dish is smashed into at least twenty pieces. Klaus is sitting up, staring hungrily at the blobs of stewed apple and pastry, even though they are now half sunk in the mud.

"Grandmother." I start again. "You will never *believe* what has just happened!"

Klaus looks desperate. His eyes are pleading with me not to give him away.

I smile to let him know that I have it all under control.

"I was skipping around the corner, swinging my basket merrily, when an amazing spectacle met my eyes!"

Grandmother looks a little bit suspicious, but I carry on.

"The pie dish had grown wings and was flying hither and thither all over the yard and Klaus was leaping up and down, grabbing at it. I cried, 'Goodness gracious me, Klaus! What are you doing?' and Klaus replied, 'I was just walking by on my way home from school, when I saw this apple tart grow wings and start to fly away and I thought I had better catch it so that Inge Maria Jensen and her grandmother

128

would not go hungry this evening.' So I joined in and tried to help, but at the very moment that Klaus leapt up and caught the tart, I accidentally collided with him and we all fell down into the mud. I am very sorry, Grandmother. As you can see, it is all my fault. Klaus was just trying to be a hero."

I smile sweetly at Grandmother and add, "It is just like a Hans Christian Andersen story!"

Grandmother sighs heavily and says, "Indeed it is!"

I'm not sure why, but Klaus's face is filled with dread and he lets out a noise that sounds like a moan.

"Well," Grandmother says, "you had better come inside, young man. A hero who has worked so hard to save our supper should be rewarded. There are two more tarts in the larder. You must join us for afternoon tea."

Klaus's eyes nearly pop out of his head. His face breaks into a big, happy grin and he runs into the kitchen after Grandmother.

He eats like I have never seen anyone eat before. He is not being greedy like I was with Angelina's ginger cake. He is really starving. He drinks a whole cup of hot chocolate without taking a breath and gulps a large slice of apple tart and cream before I touch mine. Grandmother does not seem to notice anything unusual, and serves him a second, larger slice of tart.

I pick up my spoon with the flower design on the handle and say, "Thank you, pretty spoon, for helping me with my apple tart," then begin to eat.

Klaus bursts out laughing. I think he is going to make fun of me for believing in talking spoons and jugs and teapots.

But he doesn't. He licks his own spoon and holds it before his eyes.

"And thank *you* for helping me to eat my delicious tart," he says in his most polite voice.

Grandmother chuckles as she moves around the table, filling our cups with hot chocolate and splatting more cream all over the top of our tart.

I am grateful that Grandmother has believed my story about the flying pie dish. I am thankful that she still does not know that Klaus is a thief. Most of all, I am thankful that I feel like we are a real family, just for this moment, the three of us sitting together, eating, talking, laughing.

A real family.

. . .

Grandmother sends Klaus, Fleabag, and me out to the barn to collect the eggs. I run around introducing Klaus to all the animals.

Levi is scratching his bottom against one of the large timber posts. He seems annoyed that we have caught him with an embarrassing itch. He pulls his ears back and brays angrily. Plenty is feeding her piglets and grunts a gentle hello as we lean over her pen. Hilda and Blossom blink lazily and pretend we are not there. I look around for Henry but cannot see him, so we begin to gather the eggs—from the nesting boxes, the tops of open bags of wheat, and the hollows made in the edges of the large haystack.

When we are finished, I sit down in the hay and watch Fleabag as he stalks the hens. It is a game. The hens know he is there, but pretend that they do not notice. When he leaps, they cackle and flap their wings as though they are truly scared, but they never run away. Suddenly, out of nowhere, Henry sneaks up behind Fleabag and lets loose with his loudest turkey opera ever: gabble-gooble-garble-gibble-gobble-gobble-gobble!

Fleabag hisses, leaps into the air, and runs to my lap, where he feels safe.

Klaus flops down beside me, giggling, and pats Fleabag.

He says, "Thank you for that brilliant story you told about the flying pie dish. It was very clever."

"And a very big lie," I add.

Klaus blushes and stares at his dirty knees. I wonder why he wears shorts, even though the winter chill is still in the air.

"You're so lucky," he whispers.

My skin begins to prickle and I feel all the squashed grief and anger rise in me again.

"You're so stupid!" I snap. "I'm not lucky. My papa died when I was just a baby and now my mama is dead."

He doesn't look impressed, so I yell, "My mama is dead! Dead! Dead! That means I'm an *orphan!*"

Klaus picks one of the scabs off his knees and says quietly, "There are worse things than being an orphan."

I am so angry and so full of sadness that I scrunch my hands into fists and squeeze my eyes closed until I see swirls of red tumbling around in my head. When I open them to yell at Klaus again, he is nowhere to be seen.

I run outside and call his name, but he does not answer. I run into the kitchen, but he is not there.

He has gone.

Chapter 16

THE SECRET ATTIC

Grandmother does not mention Klaus again that evening. She is too busy cleaning out the larder. She sits three jars of preserved peaches, a wedge of cheese, and five apples outside on the back step.

"They are old," she says. "I will feed them to Plenty in the morning."

I offer to take them out to Plenty right now. I know she will appreciate some extra supper. But Grandmother snaps, "No! No, thank you, Inge Maria. That is very kind of you, but I really want you to get ready for bed. We have a busy day tomorrow. I want to clean out the attic."

I am so excited at the discovery that Grandmother has an attic that I forget all about the food on the doorstep. I forget to say that the cheese and preserves do not look old, and the apples look even better than the ones we used in our tarts this very morning. I forget to ask why Grandmother has decided to clean her larder out now, when she did it only two days ago. I forget to warn her that the preserve jars might grow wings and fly away, just as the apple tart did. I forget to ask why she has also set a blanket underneath the cheese on the back step.

I jump into bed and wait for Grandmother with my Hans Christian Andersen fairy-tale book. When she has snuggled up beside me, she suggests I read "The Happy Family." It is a story about two old snails who adopt a little snail and love it as their own.

"We are like the snails," I say to Grandmother. "You take care of me even though I am not your daughter."

Grandmother looks thoughtful.

"You are not my daughter, Inge Maria, it is true. But you are my daughter's daughter, my own family, and that makes you just as precious as if you were my own child."

And then she does something that takes me so much by

surprise that I don't know whether to cheer or weep. She puts her arms around me and pulls me into her jelly-wobbly body. She squeezes me until I feel like my eyes will pop out, ruffles my scruffy tufts of hair, and says, "I love you very much, Inge Maria. You are the best thing that has happened to me in many, many years."

She is squeezing so tightly that I can hardly breathe and I think one of my ribs is about to crack, but I don't want her to let go.

I feel safe.

I feel loved.

For a moment I think, *This is where I belong.*

But then I realize that if I belong here, I no longer belong in Copenhagen. It means that I am ready to leave my old life behind. And I am scared that this is a betrayal of Mama.

I do not know how to feel.

Does belonging here, with Grandmother, mean that I no longer love Mama?

The attic hides behind a little trapdoor in the ceiling above our bed. We reach it by climbing the rickety ladder that

Grandmother brings in from the barn. It is dark and dusty and is home to a large family of mice. *I* think the mice might like to come and live in a box by the fire in the sitting room, but Grandmother will not allow it.

"They are filthy vermin, Inge Maria!" she scolds.

I am not sure what vermin are, but suspect it might be something like being a barbarian, so I do not argue. I feel sorry for the mice as Grandmother scoops them into a bucket and takes them outside, where it is drizzling, gray, and cold.

We sweep and dust and scrub until the musty smell is gone and the air is clean and easy to breathe. It is a tiny space, and the ceiling slopes to the floor, but Grandmother declares that it will do just fine.

I am confused. Fine for what? For a new family of mice to move in? Or a family of elves?

Then I realize. She has prepared a new room for Henry!

It is two o'clock and Grandmother and I are making bread.

"Inge Maria Jensen! You have more flour on your pinafore and arms than you have kneaded into that bread dough!" Grandmother cries. She is trying to be cross, but I think she likes it when we bake together.

There is a knock at the door and Klaus is peeping through the window. He must be on his way home from school.

My heart skips a beat. I hope he hasn't stolen any of Grandmother's eggs.

Grandmother opens the door and smiles.

"Good day and God bless you, young Klaus."

"Good day, Fru Bruland," he says, nodding politely at Grandmother. "Good day, Inge Maria."

I am still mad at him for running away during our argument yesterday, but he is trying very hard to be friends. He has not even called me Goat Girl.

Grandmother invites him inside and asks him to sit at the table.

"We are nearly finished our bread making," she says, "and then we will have some afternoon tea."

Klaus smiles, then whispers, "Thank you for the peaches and apples and cheese. They were delicious."

I gasp. Klaus has just confessed to stealing the scraps we put out for Plenty. Now Grandmother will know that he is the Bornholm thief! All my creative storytelling has gone to waste. I slap my floury hand to my forehead and roll my eyes.

Grandmother smiles and says, "I am glad that you found the food, child. And the blanket?"

"It's in the barn, folded up on the wood stack, thank you very much," Klaus replies.

I am confused. Grandmother and Klaus seem to have a whole different conversation going than the one I had expected. I stare from Klaus to Grandmother and back to Klaus.

"Inge Maria," Grandmother scolds. "Stop gaping like a smoked herring and get that dough shaped into buns."

She places her tray of perfectly formed loaves by the stove to rise, and pops a saucepan of milk on to boil. By the time I have made my buns, afternoon tea is served—hot chocolate, marzipan cake, and the gingerbread mice that I made this morning. They do not look much like mice, but as I explained to Grandmother, they were squashed by a broom when a cruel old lady swept them out into the rain and wind.

I sit silently beside Klaus, nod hello to Grandmother's teapot, and sip my hot chocolate.

Klaus picks a biscuit from the plate and says, "Wow! These look like mice."

I smile and forget our argument of the day before. Soon we are chatting and giggling and Klaus even joins in when I start dancing the gingerbread mice around the table to my song:

> *Clap, clap, cake.*
> *Tomorrow we shall bake.*
> *One for Mama, one for Papa,*
> *One for little Klausy.*
> *Gobble, gobble, gobble,*
> *Yum, yum, yum.*
> *Gobble, gobble, gobble,*
> *Yum, yum, yum.*

I am expecting Grandmother to scold me any moment for playing with my food, but she just sits back in her chair, sipping her tea and smiling as though she is watching the most wonderful sight in the world.

When Klaus starts to leave at five o'clock, Grandmother says, "Inge Maria, why don't you show Klaus the attic?"

We take a candle and Fleabag up the ladder and sit side by side in the cozy space.

"This will be Henry the turkey's bedroom," I explain.

"It did belong to a family of mice, but Grandmother made them leave because they were vermin and barbarians."

Fleabag hisses. He loves Grandmother and agrees with everything she says and does, even if it is nasty.

Klaus is smiling his big toothy grin.

"Henry will love it up here. I just hope he doesn't run around singing opera all through the night and keep us awake," I say. "Or fall through the trapdoor and land on our bed."

Klaus and I giggle at the thought.

"Hey!" Klaus cries. "Talking about singing reminds me. We had music today, and guess what?"

"Fru Ostergaard played so lifelessly that she fell asleep on the piano and flopped nose-first onto the keys?" I guess.

"No!" Klaus yells. "We danced! Fru Ostergaard started to play 'Come Hither Little Rabbit-O,' and before she knew what was happening, Finn, Knud, Rasmus, and I had started hopping around between the desks, and *all* of the little kids joined in."

I clap my hands.

"And then," Klaus adds, almost breathless with excitement, "Fru Ostergaard stopped playing and started yelling at us to return to our desks, but everyone just sang louder and all the big kids joined in the dancing too. Her Nielsen was laughing so hard that his face turned red. By the end of the second verse, he was clapping in time to our singing and hopping!"

"What did Fru Ostergaard do?" I gasp.

"She sat down at the piano and started playing again!" he shouts.

We both roll around on the attic floor, laughing until we cry, then laughing some more, until Grandmother pops her head up through the trapdoor and puts a stop to it by saying the oddest thing.

"Well, Klaus? What do you think of your new room?"

What on earth is Grandmother thinking? We cannot take Klaus away from his own family. That would be stealing, and we *all* know that stealing is wrong.

And where will Henry sleep? There isn't enough room up in the attic for a turkey the size of a tea chest *and* a boy. It was barely big enough for the large family of mice when they were there.

I am silent through dinner, trying to work my confused thoughts into sense.

Klaus is silent too. I wonder if he hates the soup, or if he is trying to work out a polite way of telling Grandmother that he really needs to go home before his father starts worrying.

I am just about to tell him he is excused when Grandmother says, "I think you need to tell us your story, Klaus."

I am expecting Klaus to tell a tale about a turkey, an attic, and a magic wedge of cheese, or something similar. I know it will not be quite as exciting as any of *my* stories, but I'm looking forward to hearing it nevertheless.

I nod encouragingly and Klaus begins.

"My mother died a year ago, when she was having a baby. The baby died too. Then my father got sick, and he was sick for nearly a year, and then he died in February — four weeks ago, I think."

This story is not turning out to be anything like the fairy tale I was expecting. My mouth is wide open in shock, but I don't seem to be able to close it. Grandmother does not even tell me to stop gaping like a salmon on dry land.

"When my father died," Klaus continues softly, "the landlord told me I had to leave, so I did. I walked all the way up the coast to my aunty's house in Gudhjem, but she said she couldn't afford to feed another mouth, so I walked back here again."

I think of the map of Bornholm on the classroom wall at Svaneke Folk School. Gudhjem must be nearly fifteen kilometers away, which means Klaus walked thirty kilometers there and back. And all on his own! I open and close my mouth, but do not know what to say.

"I didn't have anywhere to go, but at least I've got my friends at school."

He is almost whimpering now.

Grandmother reaches across the table and squeezes his hand.

"Where do you sleep, child?" she asks.

"In barns and windmills and woodsheds — anywhere that gets left unlocked for the night. Sometimes in hedges, but it gets really cold and I get too wet to go to school the next day. And I like school. It's warm and dry and I feel safe there."

"But where do you wash?" I ask.

"In the streams or at the pump down by the harbor," he says quietly and with a hint of embarrassment in his voice. "It's cold, and it doesn't always work too well."

"What do you eat?" I ask.

But before he can answer, everything falls into place.

Klaus is not a thief. He is not a wicked boy who gets a

thrill out of stealing what belongs to others. He is not even a greedy boy who gets fed at home and then wants to eat what belongs to everyone else on Bornholm.

He is an orphan, homeless, all alone in the world, trying to keep himself from starving to death.

No wonder he thinks I am lucky!

I look at his bony hands and dirty fingernails, then up into his skinny face. He looks sad, and even worse, ashamed of who he is.

I reach out and grab his other hand.

"It's okay," I say. "Henry is quite happy in the barn. You can have his room."

Klaus smiles, showing all of his teeth, then bursts into tears.

Chapter 17

THE FORLORN FAMILY OF MICE

Grandmother sends me into the sitting room to play with Fleabag. When I leave the kitchen, Klaus is quite excited about having a real, warm bath for the first time in many weeks. I'm sure he'll feel differently once Grandmother starts scrubbing so hard that she rubs off half his skin, and holds him under the water until he thinks he's going to drown.

I take a ball of white wool from Grandmother's knitting basket and roll it across the floor. Fleabag flies through the air and seizes it. He rolls, kicks, and scratches until the ball is a scruffled, tangled blob. I try to roll it again, but it is too messed up, so I choose another ball from the basket, a red one. I tumble it toward the bedroom and Fleabag leaps and attacks, chewing, clawing, pummeling, until it is a nest of knots.

I take ball after ball out of the knitting basket for our game until there are none left.

I stop to look around me and gasp at the mess we have made of Grandmother's precious wool. There are piles of red, white, blue, black, and green yarn scattered all over the floor. Some of it is soggy with kitten dribble, some is sooty from being dragged across the bricks in front of the fireplace, some is trailing out like long worms across the floor, and *all* of it is full of knots and snags that Grandmother will never ever be able to untie in a million years.

I run around with the knitting basket, trying to tidy it all away before Grandmother sees the mess, but Fleabag is grabbing at the wool and dragging it off faster than I can pick it up.

I am wrestling with an extra-large muddle of white wool that is tangled around Fleabag's fluffy black legs when Grandmother walks into the sitting room.

"Inge Maria Jensen! What on earth have you done to my knitting yarn?" she cries. Her big, soapy hands are sitting on her hips, but I know they are twitching to find a naughty leg that needs slapping.

"Grandmother!" I gasp. "You will never *believe* what has just happened."

Klaus appears behind Grandmother, his face clean and pink, his hair combed tidily across his forehead. He is wearing a white nightshirt that looks suspiciously like one of Grandmother's blouses, but he does not seem to mind. He is grinning from ear to ear.

I smile back at him until Grandmother growls, "Inge Maria . . ."

"Oh, Grandmother!" I cry. "I was sitting quietly in the rocking chair with Fleabag on my lap. I was telling him the story of the Little Mermaid, when what do you think happened?"

I wait for her to guess, but she just presses her lips tightly together and glares at me, so I give the answer myself.

"The entire mouse family, who you had thrown out of the attic into the rain this very morn, squeezed their way under the front door."

I glance at the door and notice that it sits tightly against the floor, but hope that Grandmother will not realize.

"First came the father mouse wearing nothing more

than a light summer coat, then the mother mouse wearing a thin cotton dress, and last of all, ten little baby mice in their underwear."

"There were *eight* baby mice," Grandmother says.

"Yes, I mean eight," I say, correcting myself. "It is very hard to see here in the sitting room with just the fire for light. Anyway, the entire mouse family came inside, looking very damp and very cold in their summer clothes. The mother mouse said, 'Oh goodness gracious me, that old woman was nasty to throw us out of our warm home on such a miserable damp day. We must find some wool so that I may knit us all some warm sweaters and some lovely, big red floppy hats with pompoms on the top to keep us warm in our miserable new home outdoors.'"

I glance at Grandmother to see if she is feeling guilty about the mice. It does not appear so.

Klaus sneaks into the room and sits down by the fire. I can tell that he is bursting to know what has happened in here.

"Imagine the mice's surprise and jubilation," I cry, "when they spotted a basket full of brightly colored yarn! 'Oh, Mother Mouse,' wept the father with joy, 'there is enough yarn here to knit sweaters and hats and even stockings for us, each and every one!' But alas, every time the father mouse tossed a ball of yarn down to the mother mouse, Fleabag leapt upon it, kicking and biting and thrashing until it was a tangled mess."

I stop, suddenly aware of a major weakness in my tale. Cats love to chase mice. Fleabag would have attacked the mice long before they made it to the knitting basket.

Grandmother walks over to the rocking chair and signals for me to come near.

This is it! I think. *I've had it now.*

But when I approach, she sits down and draws me onto her lap. She rocks gently back and forth and says, "Do continue, Inge Maria. Klaus and I are fascinated to know what happened next."

Klaus nods and smiles, his eyes sparkling.

"Well," I say, gulping, "you would think that Fleabag would attack the mice, being a cat of savage nature, but it is so very dark in here and his eyesight is poorly, so while he could see the large, brightly colored balls of wool as they flew across the room, he could not see the gray mice against the dark floor. In fact, he thought the balls of wool had become enchanted and were flying across the room on their own, which is why he attacked them with such ferocity and made such a devastating mess of them!"

Klaus laughs out loud and slaps his leg in appreciation.

I smile, excited at my own cleverness in making the story turn this way.

Grandmother rocks back and forth, stroking my hair, and says, "And what happened to the mice?"

"I know! I know!" shouts Klaus.

I glare at him. How could he possibly know when he was in the bath? But he finishes the story anyway.

"They were so terrified at the sight of Fleabag, the ferocious black beast, that they scampered into the kitchen. I saw them because I was in there bathing!"

Grandmother nods and mutters, "I see."

"And I had splashed so much soapy water around while bathing," Klaus continues, almost shouting with excitement now, "that they slipped and skidded right across the kitchen floor, underneath the doorway and back outside into the cold from whence they had come!"

"Yes!" I cry. "Exactly!"

I wink at Klaus to thank him for finishing my story so

well. I am especially impressed that he has managed to use such a charming word as "whence" at the end of our tale.

Grandmother stops rocking and says, "Well. Let that be a lesson to me. If I am going to treat mice poorly, they will return and punish me in some way or another. It will be a long day's work untangling all these knots from my wool tomorrow, but at least you will be home to help, Inge Maria. Now off to bed with you both!"

Klaus goes into his attic first, and Grandmother lets me climb up to say good night. I see that he is tucked in safe and warm amidst the pile of eiderdowns, blankets, and pillows that Grandmother has arranged into a bed.

"Thank you for finishing my story so well," I say.

He smiles.

Grandmother's wrinkly old face pops up through the trapdoor. She looks like a jack-in-the-box. Klaus and I burst out laughing.

Grandmother frowns and grumbles, "I am too old to be filling my house with silly little children."

But we both know that she is having as much fun as Klaus and me.

Klaus leaps out of his nest of eiderdowns and kisses Grandmother on the cheek.

"Goodnight, Fru Bruland," he whispers.

I have that funny feeling again, like I am in the middle of a real family. Like this is where I truly belong now.

I wonder if Klaus and Grandmother feel the same.

Chapter 18

THE RUNAWAY BLOOMERS

Klaus is annoyingly good at milking Blossom. His father used to run a dairy before he got sick. I am still yawning, trying to get in the right position on my stool beside Hilda, when I hear the sound of milk squirting into his bucket. Blossom doesn't kick Klaus once, and when the bucket is half full, she twists her head around so that she can lick the back of his neck as he milks her. Klaus keeps brushing her tongue away, but she just wraps it around his wrist, licks between his fingers, then continues to slurp at his neck.

Grandmother throws her head back and laughs.

Levi, jealous of the attention Grandmother is giving to

someone else, trots up beside her and chomps his big square teeth down hard on her bottom.

"You stupid piece of donkey flesh!" she cries. "I'll be sending you to the glue factory in Copenhagen before you know what's happened!"

Levi pulls his ears back, rolls his eyes, and brays. He is full of cheek, so Grandmother punishes him by feeding his morning carrot to Plenty. This angers him even more and he trots around the barn, kicking at posts, empty buckets, and Henry. Henry runs to Grandmother for protection, ruffling his feathers and gobbling like Chunky Jorgensen's wife on a Sunday: gobble-gobble-gabble-gibble-gobble!

Levi is even more jealous of Henry than of Klaus. He kicks his back legs again and the gate to Plenty's pen flies open. Fourteen fat pink piglets scatter across the barn, squealing in fright or joy. It's hard to tell with piglets.

Grandmother pours the best cream into a dish for Fleabag, gives Plenty a full bucket of milk in her trough, and takes the rest inside to make butter, oatmeal, and hot chocolate.

Once Klaus and I have been fed so much breakfast that we are bursting, Grandmother announces that Klaus will not be going to school today. When I ask why, she points to his ragged shorts. We can see his pale skin showing through in seven different places and the side seams are looking dangerously frayed.

"I think," says Grandmother, "that they might just hold together until we make it to Tina and Olga Pedersen's house. They own a sewing machine and know how to tailor a fine pair of pants."

Klaus is blushing and I know it is not because of the holey shorts. He is remembering the last time we were at Tina and Olga's. The time he tried to steal the eggs.

"It's okay, Klaus," I say, squeezing his hand. "Tina and Olga like naughty children."

He looks unconvinced.

I ruffle my stumpy clumps of hair and smile.

"They like me, and I'm the most wayward girl ever to have set foot on Bornholm, aren't I, Grandmother?"

Grandmother smiles at me as though she is truly proud of my naughtiness.

Viggo runs out to greet us as we come over the hill toward the Pedersen twins' cottage. He stops wagging his tail and sniffs suspiciously at Klaus's hands, but I slip him a gingerbread mouse, then two more, and he relaxes.

Tina and Olga nearly burst with excitement when they see that Grandmother has not one, but *two* children with her. They cackle and fuss like excited hens and hustle us into the cottage. They peel off my hat and ruffle my hair with fresh delight and laughter.

"Such a spirited child!" says Tina (or maybe it is Olga).

"Yes. So full of mischief and fun!" cries Olga (or maybe it is Tina).

Then they turn to Klaus and cry, both at once, "And who might this be?"

Grandmother puts a hand on Klaus's shoulder and says, "This is Klaus. He has come to stay with us and is in need of some new pants."

Klaus and I spend the morning playing with Viggo, running up and down the lane, climbing trees, and making trips to and from the kitchen, where Olga and Tina feed us and make Klaus try on his new trousers as they are being sewn. When the first pair of trousers is complete, Grandmother says we are not needed for an hour or two and may head off for a little walk.

We run across the paddocks, Viggo barking and nipping at our heels, enjoying the sunshine and the first warm breeze for the year, which tells us spring is truly on its way.

We throw sticks into the rapidly flowing creek and run along the banks, trying to keep up. We tumble down the hillsides until Klaus's new trousers are covered in mud and grass stains and we find ourselves at the back of Angelina Nordstrup's farm.

Angelina is taking advantage of this beautiful sunny day. Her clothesline is full of washing—snowy white sheets, aprons, blouses, bonnets, and the longest, skinniest pair of bloomers that I have ever seen. I point them out to Klaus and he begins to giggle. A sudden gust of wind catches the washing and the legs of the bloomers blow back and forth in different directions, as though they are running through the air all on their own. Klaus and I collapse on the grass, laughing until our tummies ache.

I don't know if it is the giggling or Klaus's company or just the beautiful spring weather, but I am filled with a wild, mischievous joy.

"Let's take the bloomers!" I say.

Klaus is shocked.

"No!" he says. "That would be stealing! And I am not going to do that ever again."

"I'm not going to *steal* them," I explain. "I'm just going to *borrow* them. I'll run across the hills, waving them like a flag, and then I will peg them back onto the clothesline. Angelina Nordstrup will never know."

"I don't think that is a good idea," Klaus says.

But I am over the stone fence and across the yard before he can stop me. I grab the bloomers and, as I make my escape, I yell, "Bottoms and buttocks!" into the breeze for good measure.

Viggo starts frolicking around me, wagging his tail and barking at the top of his voice.

"Shoosh, Viggo! Shoosh!" Klaus yells, but the dog will not obey. He likes this game and I am certain he would bark words like "bottoms" and "buttocks," and "bloomers," too, if he knew how.

The back door to the cottage flies open. Angelina spies trouble and screams in a rage.

"Run!" I shout, and head off up the hill, flapping the bloomers above my head.

I am a Viking, running across the island of Bornholm, fierce, savage, wild, and free.

Klaus, not knowing what else to do, runs after me, crying, "Don't leave me, Goat Girl!"

Angelina Nordstrup jumps her stone fence and sprints after us, waving a broom in the air, shouting, "Stop, thief!

Stop, thief!" She is surprisingly nimble for such a skinny old woman.

Viggo, sensing that we are in danger, now runs after Angelina. He is leaping, barking, snapping at the bristles of her broom as it waves back and forth.

I run and run, half screaming, half cheering, down the other side of the hill, along the creek and up and down two more hills until I am barreling down the lane toward Tina and Olga Pedersen's cottage.

Tina, Olga, and Grandmother rush out of the cottage to see what is wrong.

I am still flapping Angelina's long, skinny bloomers in the air and my clogs are splashing mud all over my skirt, my apron, my face. Klaus is running behind me, crying and laughing at the same time. Angelina Nordstrup is gaining on him, swinging the broom so close to his head that his hair whooshes this way then that every time the broom passes by. Viggo is barking and snapping, and finally, realizing that he cannot catch the broom bristles, decides he will go for Angelina's skirt. There is an almighty ripping sound that everyone can hear above the shouting, clomping, laughing, and crying. Viggo has torn the entire back half of Angelina Nordstrup's skirt off!

Grandmother steps out into the lane and suddenly I am brought to a halt. Klaus runs into my back, shoving me into Grandmother, who topples over. Angelina stops in her tracks, holding on to her broom for support as she puffs and pants and tries to catch her breath. Viggo's mouth is full of black linen skirt and he is shaking it from side to side, growling, as though it is a wild animal he must kill.

"Viggo, sit!" cries Tina (or maybe it is Olga), and everything falls quiet.

I look around me and see the consequences of my mischief. Grandmother is sitting in the middle of the lane, glaring. Klaus's brand-new pants are torn and muddied, and his face is filled with fear and dread. Angelina Nordstrup is craning her neck to see why her bottom feels so draughty. Viggo is sitting politely on the side of the lane, pretending that he does not have the back half of Angelina's skirt dangling from his teeth. And Tina and Olga are whispering excitedly into each other's ears, nodding and chirping like crickets.

I hold Angelina's bloomers up above my head to feel them rippling in the breeze one last time.

"Goodness gracious me, Angelina Nordstrup!" Grandmother cries. "They look exactly like the bloomers you wore to our Sunday school picnic way back in 1863."

Angelina's eyes grow wide.

Tina (or maybe it is Olga) cries, "My word! It's true! The same bloomers that *everybody* saw when Dizzy jumped on your skirt during the potato-sack race and ripped it clean off!"

"Oh yes!" cries Olga (or maybe it is Tina). "Absolutely *everybody* saw your bloomers . . . even the boys!"

Angelina's eyes grow even wider, and she lets out a funny snuffling sound.

"Oh no!" whispers Klaus. "You've made her cry! We're in for it now."

But her face is not sad. She is grinning from ear to ear and the snuffling is growing louder and louder.

Tina and Olga start to titter and giggle. Grandmother slaps her hand in the mud and guffaws. Angelina holds her skinny belly and cackles with glee, and Viggo drops her skirt and howls along for the fun of it.

I watch Grandmother all day, thinking that she must be working her way up to a scolding for yesterday's mischief. It is agony waiting for my punishment, but every time I try to speed things up by mentioning the long, skinny bloomers, Grandmother dissolves into laughter and cannot talk, walk, or even stand up straight for at least five minutes.

Finally, just before Klaus is due home from school, she sits down on the haystack in the barn and says, "Come here, Inge Maria. I want to talk to you."

I sit beside her and fiddle with the corner of her apron.

"When I was a girl," she says, "I was spirited and creative, just like you. I was always in trouble at school and often dragged my friends into trouble with me. Even when I didn't try, things just seemed to go wrong."

"Like when you pulled Angelina's skirt off in the potato-sack race?" I ask.

"Yes, just like that!" She laughs. "*And* the time I accidentally pushed the teacher over the fence into the blackberry bushes . . . *and* the time I taught my donkey, Tulip, to sit, and she sat on Chunky Jorgensen and wouldn't stand up again. That's why everyone calls me Dizzy. I was wild and dizzy and made everyone around me dizzy with the excitement of what would happen next."

"That's a good thing," I say, "isn't it, Grandmother?"

"You would think so. But we are told to be mature and

behave, and for some silly reason, we believe this means that we can no longer have fun. We forget how to laugh, how to yell, how to run, and worst of all, how to delight in each other's company. I think we Bornholmers have failed to notice that the same Lord God who gave us the strength to work and the wrinkles to frown also gave us the legs to dance and the voices to sing!"

"And the teeth to smile," I add helpfully, showing as many of my own teeth as I can.

Grandmother laughs and chomps her false teeth in reply.

She becomes suddenly serious and says, "When you first arrived, I was very worried, Inge Maria. How was I, tired old Dizzy Bruland from Bornholm, going to look after a bright, beautiful young lass from Copenhagen without making a mess of it? You see, your mother was just like you — smart, creative, lively. She was the joy of my life. But Bornholm was too dull for her. The quiet island and its somber people made her feel smothered and unhappy, so she left. She sailed far, far away to Copenhagen and never returned. I lost her forever."

Tears are rolling down her soft, wrinkled cheeks and she does not even try to brush them away. I lift Fleabag into her lap and wrap my arms around her jelly-soft middle.

Grandmother strokes my tufty hair and continues, "I was scared that the same would happen with you, child. You stepped off that boat looking wild and special and every bit as precious as your beautiful mama. I did not want to turn you into a dull islander, or worse still, learn to love you, then see you leave Bornholm and my life forever."

She wipes the tears from her cheeks and smiles down at me.

"But I know better now, Inge Maria Jensen," she whispers. "You are stronger than old Dizzy Bruland. You are stronger, even, than your beautiful mama. You will not be squashed or driven away."

She grabs my face between her hands.

She is smiling and proud as she says, "Just look at you! You don't need to run away or to change. You are changing *us* instead, shaking us from our dull, quiet lives. People are chattering, laughing, being taken by surprise. I used to wake gently in the morning and know *exactly* how every little moment of my day would go. There is no joy in that. *Now* I wake in the morning, dizzy and excited, with a kitten chewing on my ear, wondering, 'What will Inge Maria do today?' You have brought me alive."

Chapter 19

THE TRAVELING HAPPINESS

Klaus is home late from school. I sit on the fence and stare out across the meadow, waiting impatiently for his blond hair and toothy grin to pop up over the top of the hill.

When he does appear, he is tangled up with the Pedersen twins, Viggo, and a riot of colors. Tina and Olga are wearing their gray dresses and bonnets as usual, but one has a bright purple scarf wrapped around her neck, the other a bright red scarf. Klaus is carrying a large blue kite, and the tail of orange, yellow, and green ribbons is swirling above and around him in the breeze as he walks. Their brilliant colors paint them into one great, jolly picture. They look like a carnival coming to town.

I feel a little knot in my stomach, but I am not sure why.

Klaus runs down the slope to greet me, the kite flapping above his head, Viggo nipping at his heels. His smile is so wide and cheerful that the knot disappears.

"Look!" he shouts, words tumbling over his puffing breaths. "A kite! It is Olga and Tina's, but they have brought it over for you and me to play with."

Viggo barks.

"And you too, Viggo!" Klaus laughs.

I jump off the fence and find myself running across the hilltops, screaming, giggling, ribbons flapping-snipping-snapping above my head, a skinny boy grinning by my side, and a big gray dog lolloping and leaping around the folds of my skirt. Color and laughter and wind in my hair. Grass rushing by beneath my clogs. Noise and speed and wild joy.

I look back toward the house and see Olga, Tina, and Grandmother watching.

"Come on!" I yell down at them. "Come and play!"

And no one is more surprised than me when they start

up the hill—Olga and Tina trotting like two little nanny goats, Grandmother waddling like a fat duck.

They are coming to join in the fun.

Grandmother declares Saturday another school-free day for Klaus.

"We are expecting special visitors," she says. "You can *both* return to school on Monday."

Klaus and I are like two grasshoppers, springing up and down with excitement, as we wait to see who it will be. When Tina and Olga arrive, we are almost disappointed, but they chatter and cackle so much and bring such an enormous prune tart with them that we are quite satisfied.

When afternoon tea is over, Klaus and I ask to be excused, but Grandmother tells us to stay.

"Klaus," Grandmother says. "You are a very special boy and you are most welcome here with Inge Maria and me."

I do not understand why she is saying this. I know this already and surely Klaus does too.

"But," she goes on, "a wonderful opportunity has arisen for you."

The Pedersen twins smile and nod at Klaus while Grandmother explains.

"Tina and Olga would be honored if you would go to live with them. They are kind women and have a lovely home, which they long to share with a child. You would have your own proper bedroom, good food, and warm clothes."

Tina and Olga smile and begin to chatter over each in their excitement.

"Viggo will love to have a boy to play with."

"And you can get a puppy."

"We will take you to the beach every day in the summer."

"Olga bakes the best blackberry Danishes in the world."

"Tina is very clever at making model trains and airplanes. We could start a whole collection!"

I am furious.

"Thank you very much for offering," I say in a polite but firm voice, "but Klaus is very happy here."

I push my chair back from the table and say a little too loudly, "Come on, Klaus. Let's go out and play with Levi and the buckets!"

Klaus does not move.

"Come on, Klaus!" I yell. "Tell them you don't want to leave us!"

But Klaus stays at the table and I already know from the look on his face that I have lost him.

He fiddles with a prune until it is smeared from one side of his plate to the other.

He takes a deep breath and says, "Inge Maria, you are the best friend I have ever had, and I love it here. But Fru Bruland is *your* grandmother, *your* family. Everyone deserves their *own* special family."

He stands up, and for a crazy moment I think he has changed his mind and will come out to the barn for a kicking contest with Levi and me. But he does not.

He walks around the table, stands between Tina and Olga, and wraps an arm around each one's neck.

"Everyone deserves their own special family," he says again. "You have your grandmother. I will have Tina and Olga."

Tina and Olga almost collapse with excitement. One of the twins is blushing and laughing and crying all at once. The other is pushing Klaus's blond hair off his forehead and looking into his face with such love in her eyes that my chest aches.

And Klaus . . . Klaus just looks like he belongs, and I cannot be angry with him anymore.

Once Klaus is gone, I feel all the old loneliness and pain return and it makes me cold and sick. I bury myself in the bed beneath the eiderdown and clutch Frederik to my chest. I cry and cry and cry.

Grandmother brings Fleabag in and shoves him beneath the sheets, even though it is a firm rule that he must stay on top of the bedding. But still I cry and cry and cry.

When it is getting dark, I hear the bedroom door open and footsteps patter across the floorboards. There is a sudden flapping sound, the bed rocks, and Henry lets loose with an operatic performance.

Gobble-gabble-gibble-gubble-gobble-gobble-gob!

I throw the eiderdown back and shout, "Be quiet, Henry! I'm crying!," then bury myself again.

It is only when I hear Grandmother dragging Levi through the sitting room and into the bedroom that I think I might have cried for long enough. I peep out from beneath the eiderdown and find myself staring face to face with the brown donkey. He pulls his lips back from his teeth, rolls his eyes back in his head, and brays until he loses his voice. When he is done, he snuffles in the bedclothes and bites Frederik's remaining ear off.

Grandmother slaps Levi on the rump and drags him back through the house and into the barn. They are both yelling and arguing all the way. When she returns, I have wiped my face on my pillowcase and I am sitting up in bed.

Grandmother climbs into bed and hugs me close.

"It is hard when people go away," she says softly.

I sob, and Grandmother whispers, "It's okay to be sad when someone goes away, because it means that we are blessed. Blessed to have loved someone so much and to have had them as a special part of our lives."

I think about this for a moment and say, "If we didn't have anyone special in our lives we would never be sad. But we would never be happy either."

"Yes, that's right," Grandmother says.

"But Klaus seemed so happy to be leaving us," I cry.

"No, child," Grandmother says, correcting me. "Not happy to leave us. Happy to get a second chance at having his own family. Besides, he has not gone out of our lives. You will still see him every day at school and you will play together in between times."

I know she is right, and I feel a little better.

But I am also crying about people who go away forever.

I fiddle with the edge of the quilt and try to stop my lip from wobbling.

"Mama will not ever come back." I weep. "Never, ever."

"No, and that is a sad, hard truth that we will always live with."

I feel Grandmother's hot tears fall on my head and drip down my cheeks to mingle with mine.

"I am tired of being miserable," I confess, "but I am scared that when I stop feeling miserable and learn to live without Mama, I will forget her. It will be like she has never even existed."

"No, Inge Maria." Grandmother sighs. "Learning to live without your mama does not mean forgetting her. It means that, day by day, you learn to cry less and smile more as you remember all the good things about her. One morning you will wake up and realize that you have not thought about your mama for days, but that does not make the life you had together disappear. And sometimes, when a long time has passed, when you least expect it, you will still want to cry again—and that is all right, too."

I snuggle in closer to Grandmother and my elbow hits something hard. It is my Hans Christian Andersen *Fairy Tales*. I draw it out from underneath the pillows and flick through the pages. It falls open at "The Emperor's New Clothes."

I pass the book to Grandmother.

She starts to read out loud about the silly Emperor who loved fine clothing more than anything else in his kingdom. I am cautious at first, waiting for the horrible, prickly feeling to arrive. But when she reads of the sneaky weavers and the cloth that they say is invisible to anyone foolish, I find myself smiling and getting excited about the mistake the Emperor is about to make.

I sit Frederik the rabbit on my lap so that he too can enjoy the story as it builds up. Fleabag curls up beside Frederik, and I have that funny feeling again, like we are a real family, snuggling and enjoying this tale.

When Grandmother reads the part where the Emperor suddenly realizes that he is parading through his kingdom naked, I start to giggle, and soon we are both laughing ourselves stupid. Grandmother is wobbling all over like a bowl of jelly and I am hiccupping in her arms.

Suddenly, Henry flaps up onto the bed, fluffs up his feathers, and gobbles his guts out.

Gobble-gobble-gibble-gubble-gobble-gibble-garble-gub.

I laugh and laugh, and the tears rolling down my face are both joy and sorrow.

My mama will never share this story with me again, but

I have precious memories of the times we did, and I have a new family to share the story with from now on.

Tears and laughter.

Grief and joy.

Loss and love.

It's all right to have both.

I know that now.

Chapter 20

THE MAGIC PICNIC

It is the first day of July. Summer is frolicking across the island. The sun is shining and the breeze is warm and sweet with the scent of blossoms. We are sitting around the edge of a blue picnic blanket and the middle is filled with bread and butter, almond cake, wedges of cheese, gingerbread turkeys, and strawberry Danishes.

I smile at everyone, soaking in the happy sight and sound of them — Grandmother, Angelina, Tina, Klaus, Olga, and Viggo. Levi is tied up to a nearby tree and is scratching his bottom against the bark. Carrying picnic baskets must be itchy work. Fleabag is stalking toward Viggo through the long grass.

Grandmother pours each of us a glass of milk from the large white jug. Angelina cuts her almond cake into heavy, thick slices.

Klaus takes a strawberry Danish and stares at it through his swollen black eye. Girls-on-the-grass Thursdays at school have been great for Sofie, Elen, and me, but tough for Klaus, Finn, Rasmus, and Knud. Before Klaus lifts the Danish to his mouth, Viggo snaps it from his hand and wolfs it down. Tina and Olga fuss and chuckle as though this is the cleverest thing in the world that Klaus has just done. They love him so much it makes my heart burst with joy to see.

Grandmother says, "Inge Maria, may I have one of those gingerbread turkeys that you have baked?"

I hold out the plate and she looks at each and every one carefully before choosing.

"I am glad to see that they each have three legs," she says approvingly. "A two-legged turkey is a fine thing, but a three-legged turkey is a wonder to behold."

She bites the head off and closes her eyes in appreciation.

Fleabag dives from the long grass and lands on the

middle of Viggo's back, claws and teeth sinking deep. Viggo yelps in pain and shoots across the picnic blanket, spilling milk, squashing strawberry Danishes, and knocking Grandmother face-first into the bread and butter.

Angelina, giggling, peels a slice of bread from Grandmother's cheek and helps her sit upright once more. Levi swishes his tail, pulls his lips back from his teeth, and brays in delight at Grandmother's misfortune. Klaus, Tina, and Olga are laughing their heads off, rolling around in the grass, all over the top of one another.

I sit quietly by and watch for a moment.

Mama would have *loved* a picnic like this.

I hold my breath and wait for the hurt that lives with the memory of her, but none comes. Just a gentle warmth and happiness.

Grandmother smiles at me. Her eyes sparkle and she stretches her arms wide, beckoning.

I throw myself into her familiar, squishy body. Reach up to kiss her buttery cheek. Lick my lips. And laugh.

The End

A NOTE FOR READERS

Bornholm is an island in the Baltic Sea. It lies between Sweden and Poland and was quite isolated in the olden days. It is part of the Kingdom of Denmark.

Bornholm is famous for its sunny days, beautiful seaside villages, unusual round churches, and smoked herring. Smoked herring are fish that are caught at sea, then hung for hours in specially made buildings with a smoky fire. They taste delicious, but have a strong fishy smell.

Copenhagen is the capital of Denmark. It is an elegant city with pretty apartment buildings, beautiful parks, castles, canals, and the oldest amusement park in the world, Tivoli Gardens.

Hans Christian Andersen was a Danish author who lived from 1805 to 1875. His fairy tales were written for both children and adults. "The Ugly Duckling," "The Princess and the Pea," "The Little Mermaid," and "The Emperor's New Clothes" are just a few of his better-known stories that are still enjoyed today. His tales often contain an important lesson about life.

Danish children attended **school** six days a week until the 1970s. Sunday was the only school-free day of the week.

In **1911**, the year in which this story takes place, the world was very different from today. Girls were expected to behave differently from boys, in a quiet, ladylike manner. Children were often treated harshly and there was not the support and care for children in need that there is today.

ACKNOWLEDGMENTS

A truly blessed writer is surrounded by kind and talented people whose influence on the final tale is very real and very much appreciated. These brilliant people in my story world are:

Chren Byng, my lovely in-house editor. I am grateful that, once again, you have entered into the spirit of my story and have happily frolicked through the pages with me and my characters.

My publisher, Tegan Morrison, and my agent, Barbara Mobbs, who provide continued support, advice, and encouragement.

Mum and Dad. Everyone needs at least two totally biased fans. It's an added bonus that you double as wise old owls.

My husband, Carsten. Thank you for being my living guidebook to Denmark and for listening to every word I write. *Jeg elsker dig.*